THE FAN REPAIRER

Also by Despina Katsirea

"The Pelican" .... (Short stories)
"Incidents on mirror No 9" .... (Poetry)
"Journey to Pontos" .... (Poetry)
"Us in the courtyard with the statues" .... (Poetry)
"Elegies in the sun" .... (Poetry)
"Human Coastline" .... (Short stories)
"Mr Raymond" .... (Novel)

DESPINA KATSIREA

THE FAN REPAIRER

Abigail LTD.

Copyright © Despina Katsirea 2014
Book design copyright © Vassia Katsirea 2014

Published by ABIGAIL LTD.
10 Brock Street, Bath, BA1 2LN

All rights reserved
No part of this book may be reproduced or transmitted in any form electronic or mechanical, including photocopy or any information storage and retrieval system, without permission in writing from the publisher.

Unauthorised publication contravenes applicable laws

ISBN: 978-1-903056-52-3

Produced by Brown Dog Books
7 Green Park Station, Bath BA1 1JB

For Patrick and Vassia

1

He unlocked the front door quietly.

The wind was not cold, but fresh, rather cool, and penetrated his old jacket with small, insistent blows.

'It's expected' he thought, as he put his bags down to push the door open, 'after all we are in the middle of September, what else the weather would really do at this time? Go back to summer? It would be not bad though if it happened.'

The door opened with a light crack, so small of a noise that unless you knew what it was, there was no way in identifying it afterwards.

He took his bags from the front step he had left them and got inside. He closed the door behind him and locked it again. He did not really know why he had to do this, but always all these years in the foreign country fear was around the corner for everything. Nothing big really, or something important, but a vague, small, annoying feeling, which was always hanging inside him.

A smell of burnt onions and disinfectant hit his nostrils, everything though around had been meticulously clean. The chairs were on the tables until the first waiters would turn them down again later on, to sort out things around and prepare the room for lunch.

He went to the kitchen and left his bags on the table, he took his jacket off and put on a barely clean, white apron. One by one he emptied the bags, separating the vegetables in small piles of the same kind. The spring onions together, then the cabbage, the carrots, the lettuces. When he finished with them he started with the meat and the fish. The beef with the lamb in separate corners of the table covered and ready for the fridge, and then the scallops and the rest of the fish.

When he had finished he looked around, pleased that everything was in good order, and ready to be taken to the correct place, waiting for him to call again on them as soon as it would have been required for the various dishes of the day.

He was content now.

He put the kettle on to prepare his thermos with his tea, this it would last him until the evening. Little he cared what food, or if any, that he could have. Here and there he could pinch some of the ingredients as he was preparing the meals for the customers, and that would have been sufficient for his stomach in order not to trouble him with food for the rest of the day. Everything was fine.

Mechanically he started washing and drying the vegetables before putting them away to the plastic storing boxes, he could come back to them later.

He had come earlier today. He did not have to show up until after ten in the mornings, but he really liked to get up at dawn and get ready for the Market, especially when he had to visit, like today, the meat and fish dealers too.

Getting up very early was a habit he had learned to have since he was still a young boy. His father and grandfather were doing the same, so did his mother. Only his sisters were lazier.

He looked vaguely at the wood of the table. In many areas it was badly chipped with one or two cracks. He had suggested to the owner to buy a new, formica one, he told him that it would have also been easier to clean. He had laughed at him and told him that wood was after all better. It was pointless to bring up the matter again.

The faces of his father and grandfather, his mother's too, came quietly out of the chipped wood. He hold the carrot that was peeling now tighter in his hand. Then, they left again. Even remembering was pointless. It's better for life to be flat, no emotions, no feelings, no worries.

He continued peeling the carrot.

'I will start slowly with the soup first,' he said to himself, reassured that perhaps it was not too early to peel the carrots. 'I will prepare it until it's half done, and then I will start the beef.'

He had a meticulous system of cooking, always allowing for extra time, not only for the case that something might have happened, but because he liked to move around without pressure of time. He knew well that this was against him, as he was spending most of his day at the restaurant whilst he was only paid for eight hours of work. He sighed, realising once more that nothing really, even small things in life that are so well regulated for others, were working for him. It was pointless to worry though, things would have continued to be the same, either because he was not pushing them to change, or because others were imposing them. The bottom line in both cases was unfairness, but this could only been used just like now, for a talk with himself, and not as if it was going to change anything.

At the end coming here so much earlier than the others it was not bad after all. He had the time he wanted and liked, as the crisp and lonely streets of the town, were easy to move, and the empty restaurant was quiet and all to himself. It was noiseless outside, nearly everywhere, the buses were empty, and even the Markets had less people than they would usually have in an hour's time, and then it was of course here. Here, he had as much time as he wanted, and the ample luxury of an empty place, without anyone to order, push, insult, demand.

The crowds in town were still sleeping, the noises of the day were still ahead, and everything could be calm, concentrated, ready to be used in peace.

He did love that.

He was not a cook. Not with the meaning of this that it

was what he was doing consciously as a profession, or liked, or aimed to. He knew how to cook from his mother, he loved to watch her as a kid, and then it was when one day surprised them all by cooking the duck exactly as she did. That had caused a great upheaval at home, 'these things are only for women', his father shouted. His grandfather had thrown his arms to heaven, complaining silently to whoever was there listening, his sisters were laughing at him hiding their faces behind their sleeves, the servants fled from the scene. Only his mother had smiled kindly to him.

They have sent him to bed without any food that evening, that was the punishment that his father had chosen in averting him to continue this habit, however everyone afterwards devoured the duck.

Easily had come afterwards to do it for a living. After all that was what it could have provided him with a small salary to survive. That was what they cared for to have from him in this country. His studies, his other job back home interested no one. It was all right. It had put a roof above his head, a bed, then the days go, who cares?

He did, but even that was pointless. Then, it had come the habit, the things you do day in and day out, their continuity like a long, straight line is quiet and allows you no such feelings as regret, or second thoughts. For what? He finished with the carrots, and put them aside to take the onions.

The kitchen he was working had no window. A narrow door was opening to the back of the building, where it was a small, balcony with iron railing that they were keeping the dustbins. Sometimes, when these two were full, they had to go down some steps, to the grey yard, two meters by two, where they were keeping some more.

Empty wine boxes, and other things were littering the place.

He opened the door to get some fresh air, the view made him shake his head with despair, and returned to his onions at the table.

The clock, up in one of the kitchen walls, facing the sink was still showing seven forty. 'It doesn't move' told himself, 'still early, but I have lots of time today to prepare everything. That's not bad, it's good.'

He left the onion hanging in his left hand and opened the thermos at the table with the other. He poured tea in a mug with a lid, and resting his back on the chair took a sip and looked around him.

Apart from the vegetables on the table, the meat and the fish had gone to the fridge, and there were plates in lines by the side of the sink and bottles on the counter with soy and sesame oil, as well as other liquids they were using for the cooking. Then, he scanned the pans on the big stove, the crockery on a box, the cutlery in some half open draws, and the wooden and metal spoons, hanging in tidy rows around the cooker.

He smiled, it was strange to think that all these items around him, this space, and what he was really doing, was him, or consisted of him. He knew what he was doing among these things, at least most of the time, however there were those moments that the memory was running down its lanes, and the past was betraying him. It was then again, and then only, that amazement was coming back.

'I have to remember to listen to the eight o'clock news,' he thought.

Little he cared for what would be on them, but it was a routine he liked. He could find out what was going on with this world and this country outside his kitchen, even perhaps news from home.

'How China, would be looking now?' His eyes stuck on the tea leaves at the bottom of the mug. 'Would it be changed a lot?'

He took another sip from his tea, then put the mug down, on the table and covered it with the lid to keep it warm. He started on the onion again, his eyes concentrating on the peeling, his mind travelling thousands of miles back. 'Stupid,' he scolded himself for allowing thoughts to linger back on memories, 'too stupid.'

It was nearly forty years now, forty whole years that he was living in this land he hardly knew. Lonely years, bitter, but at least quiet, full of work and long hours of thoughts. He had come to London in the early seventies from Nanking the old Chinese capital. Even now, he could hardly understand how everything had happened. Sometimes it was looking like a dream, on others he was thinking of it as a nightmare.

He was the only son of a wealthy scholar, who was also running the local museum, 'did they called them curators at the time? Who knows.' He was sent to Canton to study, his father wanted him to take his place on the museum.

His grandfather was teaching, it was him who had taught him to read and write, even before going to school. Everything had been fine, life seemed to have no problems, no illusions, no frustrations. What had happened then? It all suddenly developed into some kind of madness. It was the young kids that turned everything the upside down. Could he still understand why? No, there was no way, no, he could not understand anything. He slammed the onion with anger on the wooden block he was chopping it.

'Sometimes it's not good to come so early here, 'why on earth all these things were coming back to my mind right now?'

However a shadow of death was there, in the kitchen, around the pans, and table, and knives, and bowls. It seemed that he liked a lot to be around there with him, the same as at home, always with him, never leaving him, hanging behind his back with closeness and devotion.

He continued to prepare the ingredients for the soup, then he got up and went to the cooker.

Some mixed noises started coming from outside, occasional sharp screaming of brakes, voices, others he could not distinguish. He put the radio on as he remembered that it was time to do it, and simultaneously filled the pan with the ingredients for the soup. He was glad to do everything in time, as the water was boiling, but it wouldn't have really mattered. The news have been really so trivial, the government was down in the polls, some doctor had given a kid the wrong medicine, the Americans were threatening with war some more countries, three more women were raped at a seaside resort of the West Country.

The voice of the newsreader was floating in the kitchen now, taking its place among the pans, the vegetables on the table, the wooden chopping block.

He tasted the soup and put some more salt. Even loneliness had become like a well used shirt in his body. 'What it would have been if I had stayed there?' He thought about it as he was stirring the liquid in the pan, 'they would have killed me like the others, that's what it would have happened.' He turned sharply his head away from the pan, as even the steam, or what image had come to his mind, were hurting him.

He continued stirring the liquid and tasted it again, 'good,' he said to himself. When it was really half way done, he took it off the cooker and put it covered aside. He switched off the cooker, 'now the meat,' he instructed himself.

He took it out of the fridge, washed it, and started chopping it. Suddenly he stopped there looking at it, his stomach turning with disgust, he was suddenly feeling that he was ready to throw up. He left quickly for the Gents lavatory, something was hurting him inside his stomach, too much pain, he tried to throw up but he could not, tried again, nothing. It was this immense, sick feeling now that was covering him.

He returned to the kitchen and sat down at the table. Shaking and feeling ill looked at the mug, the thought of having some tea came to him, and quickly uncovered the lid and took some sips.

The meat was still on the chopping board, but stretching now his back on his chair, forced himself to calm down looking at it, and take it easy for a few minutes as he was taking his tea. It worked. He had this little power of concentration to assist him on moments like this.

'I should not come here too early,' he advised himself again, 'too much time to think here, what's the point in remembering? Nothing changes life, it was what it was, and it is what it is, no point at all for anything else really.'

He took a deep breath, and putting his thoughts in action, got up and started cutting the meat in small, thin pieces. When he finished, went again to the cooker and pour some sesame oil in a big wok, then placed the meat neatly at the bottom of it. He switched on the cooker and stood on top of it waiting. As the sizzling started few minutes later, a noise from a banging door filled the kitchen. He cursed angrily inside him but hurried to see who was there.

'Why you locked yourself in again?' Said the young man who came in with a stupid smile hanging on his face.

'Don't bother me with your nonsense' replied Ching Lee, still in a long face, rushing back into the kitchen to save the meat from burning.

Joy slammed the kitchen door behind him.

'You are early for a change,' muttered the older man.

Joy was a young man in his early twenties, his parents had come like him into this country via Mongolia at the same time when those who could flee from the country were doing it without hesitation. His father was working for the local council, sweeping streets, whilst his mother was cleaning houses, that is whenever she could find a job. People were kind, but many times preferred younger cleaners than her.

Joy was really as a human exactly as it was his name. He hated school, and hardly wanted to learn doing anything in life. His parents were glad to find him a job at this restaurant in London's Chinatown. It was third rate, but not bad to keep him away from the streets. He had a joyful character and little thought, or care for anything else other than his amusement.

'Will you mince the pork for the dumplings?' Ching Lee lowered the heat on the cooker, watching carefully the meat, which he had just saved.

'Will you mince the pork for the dumplings?' Ching Lee instructed Joy again grumpily. He thought that the day had finally arrived now as with the passing of time, routine was returning slowly in the kitchen.

'Why don't you buy it ready?' Said the boy.

'You learn to do my job this way when you will replace me, if ever. I have learned to respect the people I feed, when you get it ready minced you never know what kind of meat the butcher is mixing, this way I always know what I cook.'

'Shall we do some more today for us?' Joy grinned in a smile to the older man, winking at the same time.

'We will see' Ching Lee replied.

'From what? There is enough pork for some extras.'

'We don't know how many customers we will have today.'

'Ha, on a Tuesday he will be glad to fill five, or six tables.' Ching Lee looked at the boy quietly, 'it's not good to cheat' he said.

'Who him? I say it's more than worth to do it.'

'Don't say these things, he might turn up any minute now.'
'No way, when did he show up before eleven?'
'Many times, anyway we shall see how the day goes, if there are not any customers, 'I will keep you some for home. How are your parents these days?'
'Father is not that well again. He went to the doctor a couple of days ago.'
'What's wrong with him?'
'He has a difficulty to pee,' Joy grinned again.
'Oh' said only the older man, 'and what did the doctor say then?'
'It's something there I don't know, I think they call it prosth, prostate, or something like that.'
'Ah, he will need treatment then' said Ching Lee.
'They told him something like that, and they have given him some medicines, I think he has to go soon to the hospital.'
'Ah, 'said again Ching Lee, and pour some more sesame soy in the wok.' That's a serious trouble then, isn't it?'
'I assume so,' Joy for a change was thoughtful now.
He put the radio on and started mincing the pork, covered it and put it aside. When he finished he started cleaning the area he was working on to start preparing the dough for the dumplings. He was occasionally singing with the music or drum his hands on the working surface of the kitchen tossing the remains of flour in them all over the place.
'Calm down' Ching Lee scolded him quietly, but all too annoyed that the brief time of peace had already abandoned him all too quickly today.
He returned to the wok, stirred the food for the last time, then put the lid on and take it away on another empty hob. 'Now the water for the rice 'he thought, still though subdued and sad.
He left his eyes scanning leisurely at the spoons hanging

around the cooker until he saw the first bubbles.

'Quickly, pass me that lid' shouted to the boy, pointing at a half burnt one from the heat, old and crooked, miserable looking lid of a casserole.

He said something that even he could not hear as he splashed his fingers with the hot water.

The day now was on, started and continued in the same pace. Doors were opened and closed around, as the waiters were coming, the one after the other, taking the chairs down from the tables, putting on clean tablecloths, and tiny vases in the middle, with one or two of the smallest carnations that had ever be seen, to decorate them.

When most of the food was prepared to the stage that he wanted it to be, he sat by the kitchen table and opened his thermos again. The waiters, two boys and a girl, were fussing around to prepare the restaurant for the lunches.

At eleven thirty, as Joy had predicted, Lao Ta, the owner, turned up, upright and grim, with narrow, stuck together, lips. The movement around became now more organised. He took his jacket off and went to the small room by the toilets, which was marked with a tiny sign 'Private,' that used as his office.

Ching Lee put his hand into the inside pocket of his jacket and pulled a bunch of small papers out. He went to the room and said good morning between his teeth.

'Your receipts from the shopping,' he told him, and continuing searching the pockets of his trousers now, 'and change' he told him. Lao Ta did not bother to look at him. He left the papers and the money on a black book at the corner of the desk and left.

He went back to the kitchen and out to the small balcony. The weather was a lot warmer now and the sun very pleasant. He stood there for a couple of minutes that he thought lasted longer and close his eyes.

'There is nothing to look at here,' he said to himself, folding his hands slowly around his body, trying to keep as much sunshine in it as he could. On those moments, really seconds, or even a smaller portion of time, his memory was whizzing again. Icons that had no connections, where? Childhood scenes with father and mother, granddad, his sisters, Pa the little dog, the house, the servants, then the school, adulthood, the young kids in uniforms smashing everything in the house.

They were not coming in disciplined series of events, unfolded in quiet order, they were not telling a story, any story. Then, it was again the grey wall opposite, and the dustbins which half opened were waiting to be filled. He searched for a cigarette. He rarely carried any, but he found two now in the bottom of his apron pocket.

'Good,' he thought, with a small, happy sigh. He lit it and blew out the smoke, which dispersed, around his face.

He looked at it.

'Such a small thing for a relief,' told himself, 'no more, no less, good.'

'We don't have enough spring onions,' Joy put his head out of the door.

'I bought enough for two days' he grumbled, and took the cigarette out of his mouth, holding it for a second with his two fingers and looking at it disturbed before throwing it to the small courtyard. It bounced twice and went to fall at a corner.

'You will start a fire here,' laughed Joy.

He swore quietly and went inside to look for the onions. They were ready now for the first customers to arrive later on. Irritated, he went to one of the big, plastic boxes in the fridge, covered with some cling film that was meticulously put around it, pulling out some bunches of spring onions that were squeezed the one next to the other. He left them angrily on the table, and slapped lightly Joy on the shoulder. 'You are not going to do anything worth in life if you go on like this.'

'Why don't you leave them on the table so I can see them?' Joy felt stupid that he had not thought of the fridge before.

'So you can use your brain,' Ching Lee retorted, 'if you have any that is.'

'You started now,' said the boy grudgily, he wanted to say more but decided to ignore the older man, pulled out two bunches of spring onions and started peeling the outside leaves.

2

Slowly, by October the weather returned to its usual habits. Grey skies, the occasional rain, colder days, were its basics, these only to multiply as time
was speeding up for winter.

Fewer people were out now on Sunday mornings, much more preferring to stay in bed, or anyway inside. Gone were the crowds that were filling from early in the summer mornings the parks and the little gardens at the back of the houses.

It was good to walk on these mornings alone, quiet and undisturbed by anyone.

'The Dragon's Head' was closed on Sundays, and Ching Lee liked so much to stroll in the streets, watching houses and people of this, still for him strange country that he really never made his own. He liked to walk and watch, everything around him, resting his hours of the day on the lives of others, and the things that surrounded them.

He could never say really for how long he was walking. Street after street, road after road, until he could not move his legs anymore. Then, somehow exhausted, he was trying to find his way home, to the solitary confinement of a tiny flat in Camden town.

He had rent the same flat for years. He hated removals, besides it was so little around to choose from. It was not great, but not too bad either.

It needed work, someone to put up some new paint on the walls, or replace the rotten frames in the windows.

Ching Lee did not have decorating talents, or could afford for a professional to do it for him. The landlord, to whom he had brought up the matter several times, smiled and said that he would look into it, but for years nothing was happening.

He was a shrewd, old Welshman, who owned a couple of old houses in the neighbourhood, which he had converted to tiny flats, slightly better than bed sits, and he preferred to rent them to all sorts of foreigners and immigrants,

No one really had understood why he had this preference, if it was the higher rent, or less complaints from people that had already too many other problems. However, there were times that this habit of his was met by sudden disappearances of the tenants without payment.

Life has these things, at all levels, with all sorts of humans. You gamble, you win, you lose, equal terms.

He opened the front, black painted door, and started ascending the narrow staircase that was leading to other floors from the shabby front hall.

He was only a couple of steps up when he heard the front door opening again and then kicked to close with a loud noise.

Ching Lee continued to ascend shaking his head. At the first landing only he turned to see who had come behind him.

Ann Barker, in tight jeans and a colourful top, grinned slightly when she noticed him, as she was searching for any correspondence among the few letters left at the hall table.

He seldom had anything other than bills, or some Council circular. No bank account, or activity, had protected him from the spreading of his address to hundreds of useless organisations of marketing and advertising. It was good, he liked this anonymity very much, and who knew him here?

"Hi", said Ann, lifting her head from the table,"How are you?"

" I am OK" Ching Lee replied and continued for the next fly of steps.

She was one of the few white tenants in the house and

also the only British. Ann occupied one of the two ground floor flats with occasional boyfriends. At times that she was happy she used to sing with a nice contralto voice, at others her screaming from rows with her men friends, could cover the whole neighbourhood.

These days she dated no one and she was unexpectedly polite and withdrawn. She usually had a small stall at Camden Lock selling funny socks and all sorts of weird gear, and at others she was working here and there at local shops.

Ching Lee had one of the two flats at the top, the other one was rented by Price, the landlord, to a black guy from Zimbabwe, working at the docks in London. Aaron was a quiet man, hardly around but for few hours at night to sleep, no more, no less.

Like him, had no friends, and the few women he used to bring around, were rather timid for their profession.

Ching Lee felt a pang on his left knee,

" I am getting old for these steps" he thought," I also walk as a lunatic on Sundays, as even the other days work and standing at the damned place is not enough."

He resumed his key and unlocked the door.

A tiny hall, big enough only for his body to move in it, a small sitting room two by three meters, and an even smaller bedroom, with a kitchen as small as a cupboard, with a bathroom nearly adjusted to its side for all odours to exchange place quickly.

His eyes turned around to the familiar things, scanning like a king his kingdom to detect problems, or damages, and finding nothing there really to notice. All the defects of the place, its poor looks and ambiance, were nothing but part of the same picture that he knew so well. He left the bag he hold on the table and went to the bathroom to wash himself. The splash of water to his face was welcoming.

He went again to the table opened the bag and then to the kitchen to bring a plate.

Very rarely he was cooking, accustomed at all Sundays to carry food home from the local fish and chips shop.

He sat down and poured to the plate the fish and the chips from the bag. Many times he despised this kind of food, him a good cook to eat these things dripping with fat, and hardly with any taste left afterwards, other of course than that sticky one at the back of the tongue and throat.

At other times though he was amused by it and his peculiar Sunday habit. However it was cheap food and he could find it easily at this day that usually most of the small shops were closed.

He cut a big piece of fish and swallowed it, his eyes scanning the view outside the window, few more houses there, two or three dilapidated, some others recently renovated. Then, their windows, with white, or colourful nets, others with hanging sheets for curtains.

He sighed, cut another peace of fish and chew it slowly to make room for the two chips that followed.

The sitting room had very few things, a table with three chairs, the fourth being always in the bedroom to leave his clothes, an armchair at a corner in front of an older TV set, and lots of boxes, which the one on top of the other were forming some kind of strange, modern design cupboard.

He had bought everything, except the boxes, cheap at an auction.

Little he cared for a satisfactory image of his belongings. Only the first time, after he brought them here, looked around and remembered his old house in China, the lacquered furniture, the porcelain pots and vases that his mother had spread in all the rooms, and the silk cushions on the seats.

Then, he had left down one of the chairs that he was holding, and for some minutes he stayed there, ready to explode in shouting, or crying, until all this thing inside him, stirring for trouble for so long and grabbing tightly his chest, twisting it with pain, pain, pain, was finally released.

It had left him though as it had come.

He had sat on the chair he left down and looked around him.

In that blunt moment, where everything had suddenly taken the form of a straight line all filled with nothing, he was no one, had no past, no future, and the present was no more than this void, which was filling him, and oozed inside and outside the room.

He knew nothing else but confusing pictures, pieces of the jigsaw, scattered here and there, and made no effort to collect them.

Ching Lee had plunged into the void of the present, grateful, as slowly the sharp pain was leaving his chest, and the ugliness of everything around him was covering his eyes without feelings.

He finished quickly his food and cleaned up the table.

"On a small place tidiness applies wisdom"

Who has said it?

Was it him?

Or it was one of the voices of the past. Ching Lee little remembered about this and equally cared.

A clock from his bedside table rang.

" Why on earth I put the alarm on?" Questioned himself without reply.

He got up and went to the bedroom to stop it. It was one o'clock," I must have walked today for at least four hours, what a stupid idiot I am, no rest, ever."

He returned to the sitting room and opened one of the boxes, at the top of the pile, and took out few gold ribbons and some pieces of silk fabric.

He placed them on the table and returned to the box to collect, almost with religious quietness and ceremony, an old fan.

Once upon a time this must have seen better days, but still was a most beautiful thing, faded but elegant, with silk, embroidered fabric stretched over its sticks, decorated with butterflies and birds.

Ching Lee looked at it for a few minutes in awe, and then placed it very carefully on the table.

His eyes were fixed on it with admiration still, but also in a careful study. Then, he examined carefully the pieces of silk, the gold ribbons he had taken out of the box before, and went back searching for more things that would have been better for fixing this type of fan.

When he was satisfied that he had really everything he needed, he sat down.

The sky had turned more and more grey outside, and within few minutes rain, like scattered tears, spread on the window.

His fingers were moving with dexterity and skilfully took out the shattered ribbon between the sticks, and looked on the gold one that he had taken out of the box to replace it.

'This must have been gold once upon a time' advised himself, looking again and again at the ribbon.

It was becoming darker inside the room, as the rain progressively became worse outside.

Ching Lee lifted his right hand undisturbed by the noise of the water in the windows, and lit the small lamp on the table, pulling it also towards his work, so he can see better.

His fingers thin and long, burnt on several places from the cooking, were now with the help of a long, thin tool, more like those in use by dentists to remove plaque from the teeth, trying to replace the old, completely worn ribbon.

He examined the gold one he had taken out of the box.

This, was an old ribbon too, but still in good condition. He had bought it on one of his usual outings in search of little wanted to buy items at the various antique shops. In some other times, Chinese clients of the restaurant, of the few really that knew this secretively kept love of his, were kindly bringing him some old things, like broken fans, or pieces of fans kept in boxes for no reason at all, or when cleaning up their house were finding things around.

"Give this piece from a guard stick to Ching Lee, he is usually collecting this kind of rubbish."

Box, after box, were filled now with them.

What a joy it was when a small piece of a fan leaf, or stick, or a ribbon was reaching him, what light was then shining in his eyes, his whole face lit with the happiness that touches someone at a similar moment, that rare one for which you often think,"lovely, on this moment I could really go in peace, and death becomes something welcoming because it will freeze forever the happy moment."

No treasure, of any kind, would have been so precious as these boxes were to the older man.

When there was no more room for these little pieces in any of the other boxes, he had to go down to the big supermarket and looked carefully at the discarded boxes that customers could collect. He was so fussy then, taking his time to select the correct one, that had to be new, strong, in prime condition and not suffering from the usual kicking, after been emptied, from the staff.

He would take it home then, clean it from anything, like pieces of extra paper, or other staff from inside, and then carefully line it with white paper from a roll that he always had handy.

" I'll do this first, and then when I will finish, I will do the wood, and then everything will dry, so I can do the other side, yes, that is."

The afternoon was falling fast.

He had found the fan weeks ago at a stall in Camden Lock. His experienced eye was attracted to it, stranded at the back of a shabby counter of a young antique seller. " Little he knows its value" he had thought, and he offered him five pounds to buy it, but the dealer wanted fifteen, finally they had agreed on nine, and he had returned home as walking out of a Sotheby's auction with a Matisse under one arm bought for a thousand pounds.

That was his folly. His only folly. Fans.

Noises from outside, as well as from the house and the other tenants, were reaching him like being miles away. Here Ching Lee was inside a cocoon, protected, warm, peaceful, and most importantly with everything that he most wanted around him, his fans.

Tomorrow it would be simply another day. The restaurant, the cooking, the shopping in the markets, the boss, all the others around him.

It was only this price he had to pay.

The big price, for some food, the few bills, and this flat of his, no more. However, all that was worth, simply worth for some pieces of ribbon, or wood, or silk, an old fan somewhere to fix.

The figures on the silk leaf of the fan had clothes added on them, on top of the fan fabric.

"Cantonese for export" he had thought when he had bought it, and now as he was working on it, and looking more carefully at its structure, he was pleased for that attribution to its origin that he had made then.

Some of the clothes were completely worn out, his fingers were cutting tiny pieces of the silk cloth and very carefully," here it is I made you Sir your robe", he said to the male figurine on the fan leaf that he was repairing his outer garment.

Hour, after hour, after hour, the time was gone quietly, the rain at the windows constant, continuous.

He lift his head for a minute and looked at the rolling water on the glass.

'And it's not winter yet' he said to himself.

Then, he moved his head again on a movement of pain, and slightly rubbed with his right hand his neck. Pins and needles were now spread all over his body, but after some moments massage, where still his eyes were fixed at the fan on the table, little he cared to do anything else to relieve his body, and returned to finish the job.

Darkness had now covered any view outside the window. The older man got up and went slowly to the window, pulling some sort of curtains that the landlord had hung for some privacy, after he had asked for this at least twenty times.

This was one thing he did not like, no one should be able to see him inside his room, or watch what he was doing.

He trusted no one, and certainly his neighbourhood was not known for any discreet, or of good integrity human beings.

Were not bad really, but here and there, were many whirred characters, or samples of an underworld that usually likes to frequent socially the police cells.

No, this was one thing that he always liked to protect, his privacy, his anonymity in this strange world he had come to live.

He sat on the table again, bringing along an oblong, old box, taking out some pieces of sandal wood.

Their soft smell hit his nostrils, and made him to twist them a little, as if he wanted to sniff. He put them, like he had done with the pieces of silk before, in small rows in front of him, and studied them carefully, before selecting

29

the one he wanted.

It was like participating in a religious ceremony. There were shrines and holy items, and attention to procedure, and respect, and devotion. There was no time, or allowance for mistakes. Like a priest, Holy Communion was in his hands, he had to be careful, to place it correctly to the mouths of those who had approached to take it.

Here and there the wood at the guard sticks was broken. He did not have all the pieces though. He retrieved another small tool, with a sharp end and with movements that a surgeon would have been jealous of, he replaced the pieces from the spare ones he had taken out of the box.

When nearly everything was ready he pierced slightly the new pieces of wood to match the piercing on the old ones.

The noises in the house were becoming more and more frequent, as some of the tenants that were working even on Sundays, were coming back from work.

The noises were coming nearer now.

Doors slammed, voices shouting, furniture drawn wildly.

He sat there for a while, still watching the fan.

Then, he pushed the light on the table forward, afterwards on the side, trying to find the best position, closer to his eyes, and the part of the fan he was working on again.

He repeated this movement many times as the work was progressing, always trying to have the best light closer to the tiny pieces of wood that he was fixing now.

The pieces of the sandal wood were now placed on the fan, which stretched on the table, was looking hardly any different from a sick person at a stretcher waiting to get assistance from the paramedics to threat his wounds.

His face was drawn, expressionless, sometimes every nerve in it, every vein, every cell, seemed frozen, without any purpose of any other existence than to do, and do well, what he was doing.

The day was now getting deeper into darkness, hour after hour a little life in the room, his, was passing quietly, undisturbed, and unnoticed. No harm for that. It was rather a blessing, a big one indeed, where time, benevolent and healing, goes without any fuss for life. Such life at least.

There has been life outside this small room, there have been people, and things, and situations, and conditions, and feelings. There has been a whole world, moving, turning, spinning, existing.

However here there was nothing.

The simplicity of the surroundings, the absence of any other human being that really existed, the lack of any situations, conditions, and feelings, where all but a small part of a broken fan.

It was all but some small pieces of scandal wood, a worn fraction of a silk fabric, some golden fills of a ribbon, glue, and an endless hope to succeed. To achieve putting all these in the correct sequence, the correct place, then the time for them to be restored in happiness.

Looking from the magnified glass, that he was putting on sometimes like a jeweller wears on his forehead, the little people on the scenes along the fabric, the landscapes, their gestures, the birds in the foliage, or the trees, the butterflies, or animals, the snow on the distant mountains, or the cherry blossom, all those, fake repetition of an imagination always working at whim, and never on a strict design, were but the whole world.

The faces, the little people then, were passing from the fabric to the room, to hold hands, to sing, or simply talk all around him.

The boats were waiting for them, the animals were walking around them, the birds and the butterflies, were everywhere there. In the boxes, his table, the chairs, the curtains.

The peak of the mountain covered in snow, was like beckoning him to go out and look at it. The cherry blossom was so fragrant and beautiful, he only had to stretch his hand and touch it.

There were no memories.

There, has never been, ever, any bitterness, or tragedy, or sadness, and the shadow of death that liked to sit on a chair there in the room, now had gone for long.

The world has been only a simple, open in front of him, small fan, a piece of small art, coming through old times to his hands.

And this fan was spinning the whole world around him in happiness.

He glued the pieces of scandal wood with skill and dexterity. The golden ribbon was left for the end, to go through the sticks, further down from the silk leaf.

Ching Lee bend his head backwards, and looked at the fixed sticks again.

The suspicion of a smile appeared slowly to his drawn face. Then, he looked again, and again, and again. He stretched the fan more to the right, looked at it carefully, and then with small tongues, little greater than tweezers, he took some more pieces of silk waiting in tiny rows like obedient soldiers in front of him, turned them around and put some throbs of something sticky out of a tube, before placing them again on the fan.

He looked at it, turning his head first to the left, and then to the right. The suspicion of the smile disappeared with every new look, and slit to a broader, more joyful shape in his lips. The job had entirely met his approval.

He was smiling with joy.

Once more he had repaired the pieces correctly, yes, perhaps this old and worn out broken fan, could be a good fan, and no one could have done it better than him. He was the best.

He was the very best and he knew it.

The broken fan looked now completely mended, and ready to be used again.

He touched it lightly, as softly and tenderly as you touch first time a lover. He turned his head from one side to the other. Perfect, it was ready.

" I will leave it open overnight, just in case anything goes wrong, and fold it tomorrow. That's it, good."

Right now he knew that he was the best fan repairer.

Not before, not when he was acquiring something that needed mending. Not when the faces were filling the room, and the birds and butterflies were flying around, not when the smell of cherry blossom was sending to his senses memories of old days.

But now.

At the end.

At the very end, when faces, scenes, landscapes, birds, butterflies, blossom, all returned to the silk leaf again.

When his head was drawn back and the suspicion of smile was broadening.

Then, and then only.

The rain, accompanied now by a howling wind, was beating the glass of the windows in an increased ferocity. Ching Lee got up and went to the window, draw the curtains and looked outside. The present world was slowly returning here. As he sat to his seat again he saw the curtains blowing against the blast of the wind.

'And we are not yet in the winter, what sort of land is this?' He told himself again.

'I can have my tea now' he was finally relieved.

It was getting close to ten o'clock.

The noises outside from the other tenants, returned to the room.

One more Sunday.

3

'My father is getting worse' said Joy, wiping his hands in a brownish, previously white towel.

'Does he not take his medicines?' Ching Lee enquired from the top of the frying pan.

'Yes, but the doctor has asked him not to drink when he takes them.'

'And he does' added Ching Lee, turning around a dumpling.

'Yes. My mother shouts to him, but he pushes her away. He can't go to work now from the pain.'

Ching Lee turned around two more dumplings.

'I will come and see him tomorrow morning, before work, tell him that.'

'Perhaps you can talk to him.'

'I will try.'

'He is a stubborn, older man, he is killing my mother all these years with his stupidities, he is so stupid.'

'You should not talk like this for your old man.'

'I will do it, it's the truth.'

'You are not allowed.'

'Not allowed to see it? But I do. It will be a lie to speak differently.'

Ching Lee took out from the frying pan a couple of dumplings that were ready and placed them on a deep plate.

He knew that Joy was right, but what would have been the purpose of admitting it? These youngsters should learn to have some respect for their parents.

He did.

Lao Ta entered the kitchen with a broad smile.

'We have the Embassy people tonight' he announced.

'Try your best for them' he addressed only Ching Lee.

'It's important to make them to come here again. All this time they used to go down to Jiung, the bastard pocketed a lot of money, and always bribes the small officials from the leftovers in the kitchen.'

'He also has good food' said Joy, chopping herbs now from the other end of the table.

Lao Ta send a poisonous look to the boy.

'Remind me to get you out of here next time you will use your stupid tongue' hissed in anger.

'I think that these are the best dumplings I have ever done' said Ching Lee to avoid further confrontation with the boy, 'try one'.

Lao Ta plunged his fingers on the plate and pulled one out, devouring with satisfaction, 'good, good' he said only, and left the kitchen wiping his lips with his hand.

'You are really looking for trouble, it's you that you are stupid then and not your old man.'

'It was the truth, wasn't it?' Joy shook his shoulders with indifference.

'Sometimes it's good only to swallow it.'

'Swallow, swallow, nonsense, you old people always talk nonsense. Why could I not say what is really the case here? Jiung is cooking good food, that's why he is known around here. He,' and he pointed towards the direction that Lao Ta had taken, 'is asking us to serve old food too.'

'No, he doesn't, it's against the law to do that' the older man retorted.

'If it isn't sometimes it's because of you and not him. If he still keeps open this hole is because of you, and you never want to use it for you.'

'Use it?'

'Yes, blackmail the bastard with the authorities, you know better than anyone else what he wants to buy, and what he serves, unless he is interested, like now, for a particular customer.'

Ching Lee had now taken out all the dumplings, and rang the bell for the waiter to take them out to the table.

'The Embassy's staff ordered them.'

He stirred the beef a little and when he saw that it was requiring more time, he sat quietly by the table.

He crossed all his fingers together and looked at the lino on the floor.

'You will lose your job' he said to Joy in a serious magistrate's voice, 'I don't think I will be able to do anything more for you then. Your old man can hardly work anymore, and your mother can hardly find work. Even if you are right, you are an imbecile. No one is employing you for criticism. They are what they are, and work is work. It's the same, everywhere. Do you reckon that life would have been easier if you were in China now? Or the work?

I tell you again, it's all the same. They are bosses and they do what they like, and they are servants, who should do as told.'

'Employees' retorted Joy, 'we have rights, it's not everything up to them to do what they want.'

'Yes it is. Do you think that Jiung would do differently? Would you consider going there? Do it. News travel fast. He will find out why you were sacked and he will do the same.'

'Why?'

'Why? Because he knows that next time you will open your big mouth it would be for him. No one likes to have people like you working under them. Bosses are bosses and get away with everything.'

'That's old fashioned stupidity,' said Joy, cutting the herbs now with anger.

'You will make them like powder,' Ching Lee followed Joy's movements, 'and they will be of no use then.'

The noise of drizzling beef in the pan interrupted the

conversation, and both returned to their duties silently.

'They want more dumplings on five' shouted one of the waiters, as he came to retrieve some more dishes that were waiting.

'Get the other dumplings out of the fridge,' Ching Lee turned to Joy.

He obeyed with his face still looking in total agreement with his morose mood.

'How many customers we have still waiting?' the older man turned to the waiter.

Four tables, but it's only the five that is expecting the main course, two and six have just finished it, and seven and eight asked for coffee. I hope we will leave earlier tonight.'

'No we won't.'

'Why?'

'The Embassy's staff will remain longer to collect the food from what is left in the kitchen, besides you know that we do not go before time.'

'Oh hell, I was only hoping.'

'Don't' said Joy, 'the old boss here forbids it.'

'Ha' said the other and left the room with the plates.

'You are more of an imbecile that I thought' said Ching Lee, 'I really regret that I found you this job.'

'Big deal' said the boy, 'washing dishes and cutting herbs.'

Ching Lee looked at him very crossed, but decided that since Joy was a hopeless case, no more talking could serve any purpose. However he might have said something to his old man tomorrow.

Joy needed someone to discipline him at any expense, otherwise he could end up badly. With bitterness but relief said to himself that it was not too bad after all that he did not have children.

He watched the dumplings not to be fried too much.

'What his old man can do now?' He picked up the thought from where he had left it before the dumplings, 'the poor sot is very ill, what discipline could possibly give to this idiot?'

He sighed and pulled the beef out from the pan, together with the carrots and other vegetables, they had a nice colour combination, and he liked it.

The smell filled the room for few minutes.

He poured them on the plates waiting in a row and rang the bell again.

As he had predicted they did not leave earlier tonight, as a matter of fact, it was much later than usual as the Embassy staff seemed to enjoy themselves.

They had come indeed in the kitchen, two young men they were, and praised his food. Lao Ta who had followed them, pointing him for the food. He had wrapped for them the extra dumplings, beef and chicken, the prawns, rice, as well as some spring rolls filled with red beans purée. They were actually quiet a lot of those and he was hoping to squeeze some in a bag for tonight. He had nothing left home for food. However that was not the case. The other staff had been already having supper but he was cooking, no time for this.

Lao Ta patted him on the back when they were leaving.

'They will come again, 'he told him, 'good eh?'

He had moved only his head. Perhaps Joy was not so wrong after all, but what could have happened if he knew it?

He walked towards the underground, Jiung's lights were still on, and about twenty people were still gathered around a big table inside.

'A banquet' thought Ching Lee.

'Hello there' shouted the voice behind him.

He turned around to see whom they were calling.

'You don't even say hello to us now.'

'Hello Ami, 'Ching Lee smiled surprised to the girl. 'Long time not seen, despite the fact that we are neighbours.'

'Yes' she said, 'how are you any way?'

'I am coping, no complaints.'

She was a Thai, tall and pretty girl that was working many evenings at Jiung's, serving. Her mother had abandoned her when she was four, she had no father, and some relatives had brought her with them to Britain. They raised her with their own children and now she was paying them back working as a waitress in Jiung's restaurant. She was a very nice girl with whom Ching Lee always liked to say a couple of words.

'Are you going home?' He asked.

'No, I just came out for a fag.'

'Bad habit' he scolded her.

'The only one' she smiled, 'no time for any others.'

It seemed to him that she would have liked a chat, and if he was not feeling so tired and hungry he might have stayed, but there was only one thing above all he wanted tonight, his bed, and as quickly as possible. The pangs in his stomach bothered him but hardship in life was not new, and many times he was winning over them.

'You had the Embassy people tonight' Ami said.

'Yes and they left late, I didn't even had time to eat.'

'No problem for that, we had made some more food, knowing their visits in the kitchen, now that they had come to you we have plenty left untouched. Hold a sec my fag, I'll go and get you some.'

'No, no, it's all right, I will find something to cook at home,' his pride, like a sticker from the past still had remained inside, without any use but intact.

'Don't be silly' said the girl, 'Jiung will throw it out, at least the cooked food, tomorrow.'

'Really?' Ching Lee remember Joy, 'do you throw food away?'

'Yes, what is the purpose of keeping the cooked one?'
She passed him quickly her cigarette, and before telling her anything else she disappeared inside.
He felt uneasy, suddenly the memories of the poor waiting on their porch, back at home for his mother to fill their bowls, came back. He withdraw to the side of the door, half pleased and half ashamed.
Ami came out quickly again, holding a big plastic bag that he handed to him.
'Here' she said, 'I hope that you will like our food, it will be good anyway to have your opinion. You know, Jiung thinks good of your cooking. It doesn't matter that you work for him.'
Lao Ta was not really liked a lot around in Chinatown.
He didn't know what to do.
'I shouldn't really' he whispered.
'Nonsense, I would have done the same if you had given me the food, we should really support one another.'
Ching Lee thought that Ami was a lovely girl, and on the second push of the plastic bag towards him, he took it and handed her back the cigarette.
'Thank you very much' he said and felt bad, 'I hope I can do the same, so kind of you.'
She took a couple of quick puffs and threw the cigarette to the gutter in a well rehearsed movement.
'Good night, see you around.'
'See you' he said, but she had already rushed inside before he finished.
He hold the bag and walked towards the tube.
It was the first time someone cared to give him something, all these years had no knowledge of such a thing. It felt strange.
Part of him was taking it badly, like if it was some kind of shame to accept it. Another was telling him that people are kind, and many times we should not judge their

motives, which can be very kind indeed. Ami was a good girl, why should he really analyse and bother himself fussing over something so small.

With this thought prevailing to all others, he held the bag close to his side and continued.

It was a cold, grey day, with damp pavements, and a strong wind that was moving leaves, rubbish, and the coats of humans to all directions.

Aaron, his neighbour, had told him this morning, when he had opened his door to examine the landing for some strange voices, and discovered they were coming from downstairs, that he was pleased the wind has slowed down substantially, 'last night it seemed that it was going to get off the roof and spread it in pieces all over the place.'

Ching Lee had agreed, he was wondering though what was Aaron doing at this hour of the morning still at home.

'I stayed behind to see the doctor today' he told him and Ching Lee felt immediately that Aaron could had read his curious thoughts.

'Nothing serious I hope.'

'I hit my arm unloading a ship' and pointed to his left arm that was keeping close to his body, 'it hurts on every movement,' he tried to show him.

'Please don't, you will hurt yourself more if you aggravate the pain, I hope that it is not very serious.'

He irritated himself listening to his voice that was repeating the same things.

'Give us a yell if you need anything,' at least he thought he had said something useful.

'Ta.'

'What does this bloody word really mean,' he questioned himself, everyone around here says ta, in town thank you two different words for the same thing, one for the lower, one for the better classes, weird country.'

He turned and went inside his flat again.

He was feeling tired, and some palpitations, like a bird moving his wings in his chest, mad for a quick fly, were bothering him from last night.

'I have to slow down somehow, for a little while at least.'

He looked at his watch.

'Early still to go and see my folks, eight thirty, perhaps another half hour, besides they are near. I can still be on time for work.'

He went to the window of his bedroom to examine the weather.

A young couple was walking across the road.

She, holding him from the arm, him talking.

Then, the old lady who came out of the newsagent, paper in hands, then two young men with drinks, the postman with a heavy bag that was moving from hand to hand, someone parking a car, an Indian boy in uniform, going to school.

Ching Lee watched humans and things moving outside his room, mixed with the wind, the damp, the circulating rubbish, the unfolding of the morning.

He had seen these scenes so many mornings, so many times, he felt always nothing about it. Everything, humans and things were but a flat picture, which repeating itself, was forming an integral part of another picture, and then another, and another, all in a line of life, outside.

However his eyes stuck for a little longer on the couple.

He did not know what was that made him watching them. Then, he smiled.

'Ah yes' said to himself,' the pang of love, and to be happy together.' He was surprised, how it had come to think of it.

He followed the young woman's look to her companion, as this one was chatting joyfully. Ching Lee knew that look, it had been registered somewhere inside, as coming from long time, so long ago that everything surrounding this memory was but a bunch of blurred images.

Her glance was covering now the man's face as he was talking. Her eyes had little lights, lit all over them.

Her companion was occasionally moving his right hand in gestures on the air, as even there was all the importance of what he was saying. He seemed full of energy and joy. Occasionally, he was turning to his left, to look at her, as her long, blonde hair were blown by the wind around her face.

His eyes had also lights, sparkling, like those new ones in a Christmas tree.

Ching Lee smiled again, 'one can smell their love from miles.'

'The pangs of love,' said very quietly and he watered his eyes unexpectedly, still watching the young couple as arm in arm were walking in the opposite pavement, until he lost them from his sight.

Why he thought of that?

He was still watching the void in the pavement now, where they were before, and stood there with all those pictures getting more and more inside his head, until, slowly, started to make some sense of them, the one was following the other, images of people, situations, movements, feelings, lost in the passing of time, like nothing.

He had been where they were now.

It's remarkable how quickly the brain and the heart discover things to hurt you. The memory snaps from small images like this, and drugs you down to more, and more, and more.

And the heart is aching.

They were going to marry soon, him and his sweetheart, Pang –Mei.

She was so fragile and elegant, her long eyelashes

shadowing her face so often, as she was keeping down her eyelids.

Her image wrapped up in a silk gown with parrots and lilies all over, her long trousers, and her hair gathered up on top of her head like a crown.

The small mouth, the smile and soft talk.

'What on earth has happened to her? What on earth? Where could she be right now, is she alive?'

He brought his hands to his chest, as even he was trying to stop his heart from even more palpitations.

His parents had pushed him out of the house from the back door, as soon as the youngsters got in.

He wanted to stay, to fight with them, but he was pushed out with some money in his pocket that nearly violently they had pushed there, a coat rapidly thrown to his shoulders, no more.

He could hear them still as he was running away, to break things, and shouting at the top of their lungs. They were younger than him.

He had ran and ran, and ran, wherever the thought of the moment was advising him to go, avoiding the big streets, the gatherings of people, trying not to attract attention. They were really everywhere, it was a miracle he had escaped.

He had reached an old servant's house in the afternoon. He was living in a hamlet, outside Nanking.

The good, older man had been serving his family for two generations, but he had grown old, ill, too tired to do anything anymore. When his wife died, he had left them for his village, taking over his parent's derelict house. It was mostly a hut.

He had given him some food, left him to rest a while, and at dawn sent him secretly on a cart, to head for Hong Kong.

'You old fool,' Ching Lee scolded himself for allowing

everything inside to walk down to memory, 'you old fool,' and he decided to get out to see Joy's father, as he had promised, earlier.

A voice was fighting inside him, it was the same voice he was carrying around for all those years, and it was always asking him for things.

Why he had not go back, why he had not tried harder to find out more. Only the older man had said that they were all gone. 'What about Pang-Mei? What about her? Was she gone too?' The older man did not know. He had gone for his sake back to the city. The house has been looted, then set on fire. His mother and sisters had refused to go, they preferred to go down with what they knew as their world, his father was dragged to one of the main squares with others and killed in front of the crowd. It was a constant punch to his stomach this strange thing inside, that image, ugly, hanging on everything, why?

He grabbed his coat from the chair and put it on with anger.

It was not necessary all this.

The voices from downstairs were multiplied, furniture was dragged through the main hall.

'New tenants', he thought, 'let's see what kind they are going to be these ones.'

When he went one more landing down on the second floor, he bent from the balustrade to look.

He could see men carrying a bed now. A thin woman was giving instructions where to leave the bed inside.

He left the balustrade and continued descending. When he reached the front hall the removal people made some room for him between furniture and boxes left there, to go through.

'We apologise for the mess' the thin woman confronted him coming out of the door in the ground floor flat, 'but you see we have just arrived'

'It's OK' said Ching Lee, and looked vaguely inside the flat.

Two little boys were running like mad in the sitting room, shouting and playing. A short man in his forties was manoeuvring something like a wheelchair around, Ching Lee could not see very well from where he was.

'More children to shout all day,' he thought in despair, which could not been of course taken into consideration from anyone.

'I am Helen Morton, 'said now the thin woman, stretching her hand to him, in a polite, soft voice, which was coming in such a beautiful antithesis with all that poverish and strange environment of the house.

She was very tall and slim, her brownish hair were freshly washed and tight on a knot at the back of her neck. He thought that she must be in her late thirties at least.

Ching Lee looked at that stretched hand not knowing what to do about it, the whole attitude of this woman was so different from all the others there, and how the older man was accustomed to behave with them.

He decided that he finally had to stretch his to her too.

'My name is Ching Lee,' he said quietly, 'I live in the top floor.'

'Please, come and meet the rest of the family,' she insisted now, grabbing him politely from his arm and directing him to the hall of the flat.

He resisted that, he did not know why he had to do it, but the whole thing was putting him now into a situation he did not know.

'Another time,' he said, 'I am sorry, but I am in a hurry now.'

The short man was pushing the wheel chair towards the front hall. A girl with light brown hair, like her mother's was sitting in it, with some kind of doll in pieces on her lap.

'It would be better to leave Abigail's chair in the hall' said to the woman, 'she can be occupied watching the removal, it might have some interest for her, besides she is not going to bother us moving her all the time inside.

Ching Lee looked carefully at the girl, the last phrase of her father lingering more in his mind. She must have not been more than ten, her legs hanging lifeless to the metal frame support at the bottom of the chair. She was carefully dressed and tidy, her hair combed into a small ponytail.

'There are always worse things in life' advised himself.

'This is my husband, Berty' continued Helen Morton, pointing to the short man now, 'and that's my daughter, Abigail,' the smile disappearing from her face. 'I have two more children, they are my boys, Thomas and Elliott, you can hear them now playing inside. They found you know the empty rooms, and are enjoying themselves. They are all right,' she said the latter with rather apologetic tone.

'Welcome all to the house' said Ching Lee, with a small suspicion of a smile, 'I hope that you will have a good time here. I am afraid though, I have to go now, I am expected you see.'

Abigail raised her head from the doll on her knees and looked at him. The older man met her eyes. It was a quiet look, rather sad for the girl, from his part, totally blank from hers for him.

The boys were shouting now at the top of their voices inside, littering the half empty space.

'I am Berty by the way,' the short man came forward to shake his hand.

Ching Lee was completely taken back by the polite attitude of this family, something that his long experience of living in this house taught him differently.

He had zero interest on all of them, but their kind disposition was inviting to threat them well, or at least that is what he thought.

'If there is anything I can do for you, please let me know.'
He said this obligingly to their good manners.

'Thanks' said Helen, 'we are new in this part of London, so you don't know, we might need it.'

He smiled and left them among their boxes and pine, old furniture, to wonder around the small flat as to what goes where, and giving instructions to the removers.

'Nice people for a change,' he said to himself, 'let's hope that they are really what they seem to be.'

It was not a very cold day, only damp, one of those that you feel you are naked down to your bones, as the dampness penetrates your body, leaving it aching and crippling.

It had been difficult at the beginning to live in the same house with all these characters that Price was usually gathering. However his situation allowed little choice. Usually, everyone there was some kind of a worn jigsaw, flaking and worn out, impossible to match with the others. Ching Lee though believed, that if he could keep to himself, it would not have been a great trouble. He could not see any other way around it, and the passing of the years proved him right.

Only with Aaron would very rarely, like today, exchange few words. With the others he had, even if that, an occasional greeting, or not, depending on their mood, as with Ann Barker.

It was not that he disliked living with others, he loved that before, his house was always full of people, family, servants, neighbours, friends, no, that was not the reason. But he did not like to mix with this strange lot gathered here,
their casual rudeness and lack of manners, was not something that he could tolerate.

It was as if what he had learned in the past was well

hidden inside, but never really gone, that polite attitude, the respect, the principles, all those vague things that never managed really to interpret, but nevertheless had managed to be part of him, like a second skin to his body he carried around all his life.

The wind was adding to the dampness an impossibility of keeping any warmth to his body.

He was feeling depressed, didn't know why, didn't know how, but suddenly was feeling that his life was not leading anywhere. He laughed cynically on the thought, like the fox that leaks her wounds. 'Where really life can lead you at seventy?'

He took the first turn right and walked a couple of blocks down to Joy's father house.

'It's always better to do only work and never think.'

Hu came crawling to open the door.

He was rather tall for a Chinese, with a fat chin, folded in pleads, two bloodshot eyes, and a hard complexion.

'I came to see how you are,' said Ching Lee, 'Joy told me yesterday that you are not feeling very well.

He passed inside the house that smelled some kind of boiled cabbage, mixed with urine.

'Are you alone?'

'Joy is still sleeping' he informed him, 'I'll wake him up for work in a while.'

Ching Lee sat down in the only chair that was not covered with clothes.

'My wife does not have enough time for this,' Hu said and showed the other one the mess around.

'No problem.'

'Would you like some tea?'

'No, I am OK.'

Hu moved some blanket from the old sofa and sat down.

'How you feel? You do not go to work now I think.'

'No, I am in pain,' and he showed the other his front parts,

49

'sometimes is really excruciating.'

'What the doctors say about it?'

'It's cancer,' he said, lowering substantially his voice and looking in fear towards the next room where Ching Lee thought that Joy might be sleeping, in case he might be heard. 'No one knows here. It's better.'

'Are you certain?'

'Three doctors said the same. However it's better if here do not know.'

'Why? You should have told them, don't you think they have a right to know?'

'No, I don't. This is my life, they will be OK without me.'

'Is it' Ching Lee hesitated, 'did they say if it is serious?'

'Very, a couple of months.' He stopped looking vaguely on the floor. 'It doesn't matter' he added, sooner, or later, we all go there.'

'So, is that why you drink then?'

Hu looked at him rather bewildered.

'What else can I do then?'

'We can see another doctor, I will take you there, perhaps we can go private.'

Hu turned his head back, and completely indifferent to the noise he was creating, exploded into a hard laughter. 'There are all the same' he said when he came back to his usual self. 'They like to play God, only they do not know exactly how.'

Joy appeared on the door, rubbing his eyes from the sleep.

'So you came,' he said to Ching Lee, 'I will make a coffee and we will go together.'

'All right'

Hu went back to look on the floor.

'Is it not anything I can do to help?' Ching Lee was short of words, those at least he was preparing to tell his friend.

'Look after him only,' Hu pointed towards the direction

that Joy had left the room. 'He will find his way one day, but right now is a bit confused, don't be too hard.'

'He needs some discipline, but I am not prepared to give it to him. He upset Lao Ta yesterday. He will not hesitate to sack him if he will not keep his opinion to him.

'He has his mother's tongue, too late to do anything about it now, I can't.'

'I will try to advise him, many times he mocks me rather than listen. I have no more power to get him another job.' Hu fixed his eyes again on the floor. 'He might be better to take his mother and go back home, now things have changed, and perhaps he can get a better job.'

Ching Lee shrunk his shoulders, nothing from what he had come to do materialised, he was depressed with the news, and there was nothing that he could do to change things. He moved uneasy in his chair, and for a couple of minutes no one said a word.

It was only Joy who had broken the silence, showing at the door of his room fully dressed for work now.

'I hope he will listen to you, 'he said to Ching Lee.

Both men looked at him, no one found to say anything

'I have to go now' Ching Lee said to Hu, rather relieved that he could leave, 'still, if there is something I can do, let me know. I will come to see you again.'

'Don't put yourself into trouble,' Hu hang a little smile on his lips, and his friend thought as he was headed with Joy to the door, that death was already inhabiting the room.

4

The sun managed to get out quiet early this morning.

It was only eight thirty and already was covering everything with light.

The sky had a gorgeous, blue colour, and the day was filled with a crisp and clear cold, which was both penetrating, and purifying from the sickness of damp all those days ago.

Even Ann Barker was in a good mood this morning. 'Actually' Ching Lee thought, 'it has been a time that she was continuously in a good mood, as even and the fact that these days she had no boyfriends around, suited her more than when she had. Some people are better to be by themselves, loneliness many times bring the best out of you, especially if you know how to use it.'

He was happy with the thought, as loneliness was filling his life too, and had no many complaints for it.

He walked down the road to the tube station, and looking at his watch he realised that again he would be earlier than anyone else at the restaurant and decided to walk at least two more stops before getting in the underground, just to enjoy some fresh air and the beauty of the day, before entering the gloom and grease of his kitchen.

'Two weeks on and the Morton's seemed to be exactly what I first had thought of them.'

Walking slowly he liked to keep up conversing with his inner self, the kind of talk you usually have with an intimate friend, with whom you may talk about everyone, and everything.

'I wonder really about little Abigail, if she speaks, or so at least I hope she does, her mother would have told me otherwise, but she just looks at you, and then you disappear completely from her, as even and her eye sight cannot really incorporate your picture, with other people and things around her, as even you do not exist for her at all, strange. Poor thing, who knows the pain she must have been in, paralysed for life, what a life, what a prospect of the future, always to be in need of someone around her to push her chair, so hard. What is going to happen when her parents die, both of them, who will look after her? Will her brothers bother to help her, or they will look after themselves, and their own families? No one really can expect from them to bury their own lives for a handicapped sister, would they? What a prospect for a future there indeed.'

He felt sorrowful with this conversation, and soon cursed himself that he never said thank you to life for having a good health, ability to work and occupy himself at this age, walk out and enjoy the day, and the sunshine.

This made him suddenly full of a strange energy, the one that optimism for everything usually injects in you, and the acceptance that you have been from the lucky ones to have what others were lacking for good.

He changed his pace into a vigorous one now, and passing some shops, he looked with interest to their windows, no matter what they were displaying, only because the whole of this grateful feeling had inspired him with joy.

From casseroles to wooden toys, and linen, everything really there was included to this new spectrum of interest. His body reflected in the shine of their glass, was coming back to him, providing him with a picture of a medium size man, with still all his hair, whose grey colour was only just a colour, without adding anything to age, still an energetic and slim body, and two sharp eyes, on which this morning the joy of life had made nearly as shiny as the glass they were reflected in.

He bought a paper at the nearest newsagent, something

that he only used to do in the rare occasions of a disaster in this country, before or after elections, and in cases of international catastrophes. For the rest of the time he had zero interest in politics, the occasional crimes, which seemed to multiply themselves day by day, the waffling of all politicians, the amazing repulsiveness of some news from TV celebrities, the endless advertisements, and the small columns of repetitive journalism.

Today, he suddenly wanted to read everything, all those he disliked and more, as them and him had formed some kind of a new bond, and he had become in full capacity a member of this country he hardly knew, and its society. Good.

It was a wonderful day to waste at work.

One of those that life, even at its low, was a joy to go through.

Ching Lee looked at his watch and calculated that he still had time to take the tube one more stop further.

'I will be tired when I will arrive, and then its all that standing nearly all day. It doesn't matter though, it's good to walk, exercise, exercise,' he retorted to himself, and laughed on the thought of the latter.

Mickie was a short and very fat man in his middle thirties. He had been working for Zhung, a rich Chinese tradesman, that always used to come to the restaurants of this area, later only in the evenings, wearing a camel coat in the winter, and a same colour raincoat in the autumn and spring.

No one had ever seen him around in the summers, and the rumour was that he was spending them in the south of Italy with some of his numerous girl friends.

Zhung liked to honour not only one, but all the restaurants of Chinatown, and especially those that were known for good, grilled pork dumplings, and Lao Ta's, because of its cook, was certainly one of them.

Mickie entered the kitchen followed by Joy, who was making signs mocking him behind his back.

'Welcome' said Ching Lee, without raising his head from the oven as he was now pulling out a tray.

'Ah, what are you cooking there?' He asked with his eyes on the oven tray that Ching Lee was now holding, looking around as to where to place it.

'I have just finished roasting a duck' replied.

'Good, good, it smells well,' said the fat man and his eyes watered more than his mouth on the full sight of it.

'Would you like a piece to try?' Asked Ching Lee, whilst Joy's signs were more and more eloquent to get Mickie out of the kitchen.

'Ah, that's good, good, yes.'

Ching Lee placed now carefully the big oven tray on the working area at the side of the cooker, and slowly in order not to burn his fingers, cut a piece from the roasted duck, and placing on a piece of kitchen towel he cut swiftly from the roll on the wall, offered it to Mickie.

He swallowed it all at once, and bulked his eyes almost immediately, opening widely at the same time his mouth, from which the steam of the hot food was now coming out.

He put his hand in front of it, forming with his fingers some kind of fan to cool it down.

Joy's face was lit with pleasure and amusement, as Ching Lee was watching Mickie with indifference.

'You should have not swallowed it immediately, couldn't you see that it was hot?'

'You should have told me,' shouted Mickie, still airing his mouth, as two tears were rolling down his fat cheeks. 'You are trying to kill me.'

'I Told you, I told you, you tried to kill yourself. You could see it was hot, couldn't you?'

Mickie was known to all at the restaurant, because apart

from his great appetite for food, to the great satisfaction of Lao Ta, as he was watching him ordering the one course after the other, he was a frequent visitor to the kitchen for leftovers.

His only difference from the various second rate officials working in town to various jobs, was that he wanted only the good parts of any food left.

He pulled the only chair in the kitchen from the table, and sat down.

His coat, which he had dropped on his back, in a true style of Al Capone, according to Joy's remark, had now fallen on the floor, but he made no effort to collect it.

Ching Lee signed to Joy to pick it up, and put the tray back into the oven. Joy obeyed the order and threw the coat on the table, next to where Mickie was sitting, indifferent if any kitchen items, or food, left there, might stain it.

It took Mickie some minutes before his mouth returned back to normal, and he managed to close it.

Joy was watching him still with this maliciously amused look that was filled from his antipathy for the man.

Ching Lee was carrying on his work as before, totally undisturbed from both, Mickie's misfortune with the hot duck, or Joy's amusement.

'Zhung has a job for you,' Mickie finally discovered that he had come to the kitchen this time not to sample food, or collect leftovers, but with a small mission from his boss.

'What kind of job?' Asked Ching Lee, trying now some vegetables, to see if they were done, that he was stirring in a small pan.

'You repair old things, don't you? I mean, all those daft things that women use, fans isn't it?'

Ching Lee continued to stir the vegetables, pretending he had not heard, whilst something ticked inside him, suddenly in his chest, like if someone had discovered something bad about him, something he had been trying to hide. Very few knew what he was doing back on Sundays at home, and more one, Joy's father, who had given him long time ago, some broken fans that his wife had brought home from the house she was working.

Hu knew about his job in China too, his studies. They had first met few days after they had both arrived from Hong Kong. Isolation and desperation about their situation had brought them together at the time, Ching Lee had not met other Chinese fleeing home from all that it was happening there, so they had become friends, then used to speak sometimes about the past..

Ching Lee remembered that Madame Luo, Hu's wife, was lamenting over the fans of how beautiful they must have been in their time, and why westerners treated so badly such delicate items, and what a shame it was to see them at their present state.

He had taken pity of her and fixed them well.

'Oh, that stupid, big mouth of people.' Ching Lee thought.'
But who then has told Zhung? It must have been surely Joy, passing all that to Mickie at some stage. Antipathy, or not, Joy's mouth had no limits.'

'So, what about it?' He asked Mickie, continuing his stirring.

'Zhung has few of those things for you to fix. He will pay you. You see, they belonged to his family and have been damaged for sometime, he wants them fixed now. Well, he will pay you as I said again, why then not make some more money from what you get here?'

'What, more than his salary here?' Joy suddenly got interested on the matter, as well as surprised with the proposal.

'No, I did not say anything like that,' Mickie got a little uneasy, 'but that Mr Zhung will pay for the job.'

'Who said that I do these things, and that I can do the work well?' Ching Lee abandoned now the vegetables and turned to face Mickie on the subject for the first time. Joy looked quietly at the floor.

'These things are no secret' Mickie was happier now that the money matter was not an issue.

'You studied this among others, didn't you? I was really shocked to find out that you have been to the University. Not easy to swallow, that is if one looks at what you do now.' He laughed with a small, idiotic laugh that showed a gap on his front teeth. His fat face, illuminated a little by the laugh, that enlarged the width of his cheeks, showed real surprise still for Ching Lee's previous occupations, as well as irony for the loss and the fall that the other had sustained.

'Could you have found anything else to do?' He continued. 'I mean, no offence, you cook well, but with all that you had before, perhaps you could have found anything better to do.'

'If that was the case, I would have done it,' said Ching Lee wryly, and eager to stop him and his nosiness there and then. 'What is that he wants fixing?'

'Four fans,' the conversation at last was focusing on the subject.

'Bring them tomorrow morning, be here before I start preparing the lunches, ten thirty the latest, OK?

'Ah, 'said Mickie, who looked now rather astonished from the swift turning of their talk, 'ah, I will be here.'

'I will tell you the price then, when I see them.'

'Ah,' said Mickie again, and finally remembered to collect his coat.

'Will you do dumplings tonight?'

Ching Lee turned around again and looked at him with disgust.

'I always do' he said.

'Mr Zhung might come.'

No one gave him a reply, and realising that he had no more time here to enquire about food, since his mission had been completed, left the kitchen.

'Pig, 'said Joy, pleased though that he had not said much about the information he had provided him.

'You are not better than a pig yourself,' Ching Lee said, stirring again his vegetables. 'Go now to check on the toilets and wash afterwards your dirty hands,' he raised his voice on the tone of an order that was both intimidating and frightening.

Joy had no other option, but deep inside he was pleased that things had not turned sourer for him.

He had betrayed his father's and his benefactor's secret, for no good reason at the time, other than gossip, 'however' he thought, 'why he is mad with me, after all he is going to make some money because of that.'

He left the kitchen with a raised head.

Ching Lee followed him with his look until he reached the door. He was not mad. He could not be, and in reality was not so hurt that his secret work had been out. Joy was not bad, only a very foolish, young boy, with all the problems back at home. 'He cannot have any good future, if any.'

He was sad, very sad, and bitter only.

He plunged his spoon and took out a bean, and a piece of chicken, he tried them.

'Good' he said to himself.

He turned off the cooker for the time being, and left himself there, with the lid of the pan still to hold on his right hand.

Time at the present moment had disappeared again, and like in news reel, the pictures in his mind were following one another, with clarity and accuracy.

The school, the University, his good clothes, the museum.

The hours, all those hours studying and working, the long table in his room covered with books and all those tiny instruments, the pieces of mother of pearl, ivory, wood, silk. He wanted to try, he was not satisfied to be only a curator, no, not enough, he wanted to try his hands too. He adored fans, making them, learn to fix those, which had been worn, or damaged with the passing of time, was his hobby, his greater love. Dedication entirely, devotion to the point of madness.

The hours for the lessons, the long and humid days of the summer, his father serious and authoritative in his dark clothes, but also sweet and understanding.

The hopes.

Always the hopes.

And the dreams.

Everyday the dreams, for the career, the work, the life, Pang-Mei, a house, the two of them.

'One sweet and sour pork, one duck, one chicken with cashew.'

One of the waiters stormed into the kitchen.

He looked on the stained tiles behind the cooker, and put the lid back to the pan.

'Coming' he said.

The evening was very cold.

As Ching Lee got out of the tube near his neighbourhood, a strong blow of wind passed through his clothes, penetrating his skin and touched him deep in his bones.

He hurried up on the thought that the brisk walk will keep him warm, but it was not really of any use.

The house was quiet. Nearly midnight, and it seemed that all the banging of doors, shouting, swearing, having a row, or a loud laugh, had ceased at least for the few hours of the night.

He tried not to make any noise, and going up the steps, avoided using those places in the staircase that he knew the wood was creaking.

He was carrying two bags tonight, one with some food, and the other with the four fans.

Mickie had come promptly into the restaurant today, exactly on the time he had asked him to do yesterday. He had come straight into the kitchen, and found Ching Lee alone, as were both hoping.

The restaurant was very quiet, as Lao Ta was not showing up but long after eleven, and only Mario, one of the waiters, had come, and was now sorting out the tables to be ready for the lunch customers.

Mickie had placed the bag on the table, full of unwashed still vegetables, as Joy was late again, and prepared to open it.

'Wait' shouted Ching Lee, 'you can damage them more by not be careful how to handle them.'

He opened a draw and took out a clean tea towel, pushed some vegetables aside, and placed it on the table. Then, slowly, he took the bag from Mickie and took out the fans, the one after the other, placing them carefully on the towel.

'My, my, my!' He said, his eyes opening more and more as he was staring at the fans and examined them.

'What beauties we have here!'

'Ah,' said Mickie smiling, 'can you do them?'

'Watch the door' said Ching Lee, suddenly awakening from his admiration, and becoming aware again of all possible intruders to the kitchen.

'Ah,' said Mickie, moving closer to the door.

Ching Lee had bent over the fans, holding them lightly and turning them around to the light.

'You said that they belonged to his family?' He asked Mickie.

'Ah,' replied Mickie again, taking a great satisfaction in avoiding to use any words frequently.

'Some excellent pieces his family had!'

The other said nothing, but he was only watching him, and occasionally the door, his mouth aghast, wondering how he could secure a cheap for the repair price, to tell his boss.

'Well?' He said only, after Ching Lee was lingering in his examination.

'I will need some materials,' he said finally, 'I am not sure if I can find them. These are excellent pieces not to do them properly.'

'They are some spare things in the bag,' Mickie told him, 'look more carefully inside', and Ching Lee opened the bag again, to find at a pleat, undetected before, a box, which when he opened it, was full of bits and pieces, some obviously that had come out of the fans.

'They need quiet some work. I will try to see what can I do with them.'

'Will they be OK?' Mickie started feeling uneasy now.

Ching Lee raised his head to look at him, to his fat, oily face, filling with disgust every cell in his body, as he was doing this.

'I have done this for ages' told Mickie, who sighed with relief, finally reassured that the job could be done.

'I want hundred fifty pounds though, it's a difficult and delicate job.'

'Hundred fifty pounds,' shouted Mickie, 'to fix four fans?'

'Hundred and fifty' repeated Ching Lee, 'otherwise take them away and leave me in peace to do my job.'

He was more than keen to do them. His expert eye had realised that these fans were more than three hundred years old, the sticks decorated with mother of pearl, and the guard sticks with small stones, some of them he thought quiet valuable.

'Hundred and fifty' he said again, however he was not inside him still quiet certain if this was the correct price.

In reality he did not have a clue, but he thought that it was not bad to start from this, 'either you agree now, or not, after all he knew that Zhung had lots of money and he could afford it.'

Mickie looked at him. His expressionless face was betraying seriousness, however little he knew about this business himself, only the gossip of Joy had brought him to Ching Lee, and he was afraid of his boss in case they were not properly fixed.

On the price he knew nothing, but he always thought that you should bargain for everything, this is only when any trade is worth for.

'Well?' It was now Ching Lee's turn to ask.

'Hundred.'

Hundred fifty, you are wasting my time.'

'It's a lot, how can I tell Mr Zhung?'

'That's your problem. Take them anywhere else and they will double the price.'

'OK,' said finally Mickie reluctantly, knowing from the other's attitude that the cook would have not accepted anything less, 'Hundred and fifty.'

'It's a deal, and I will let you know when they will be ready, I can only work on Sundays.'

The last steps of the staircase, near the top, were creaking at all parts and even with the lightest movement of the feet the noise they made came out loudly. He hurried to his door and stamped on a small parcel left on the doormat.

'What on earth' he said shocked.

It was wrapped in foil, very carefully, and bind with a narrow, red ribbon.

He opened the door, jumped carefully over it, and went inside to leave the bag with the fans carefully on the table, next to the one with his food, and then he went again to the door to retrieve it.

Taking it to the kitchen, he noticed that it was something soft, and opening it, he found surprised a whole chocolate cake.

He stood there for a couple of minutes, not knowing from where it had come from, or why.

It was only when he concentrated more that he saw a small piece of paper that had fallen on the floor, perhaps when he was unwrapping the foil.

'I was baking some for the children, I thought you might liked to try it too.

Helen Morton,' was on the note.

Ching Lee stood there, tired from a long day's work, looking vaguely at the cake and the paper, still not knowing what to make of it. He did not know if he had to think about this present, or if he really should.

Human gestures of this kind were unknown to him, and he was very uneasy if he should have accepted it, or not. He had no friendly contact with any of his neighbours, other than the occasional one word, or two about the weather, or some common affair for the house they were sharing, and now this family comes and this woman is kind to him. 'It would have insulted her to return it tomorrow, not accepting it that is, wouldn't it?'

He had no one to answer this question he put himself, and after all the cake was looking pretty, and he was very hungry.

He took out a plate and transferred it with the cake to his only table.

'I have to do something for them now,' he told to his idol in the mirror of the bathroom as he was washing himself, 'ah it's such a nuisance to go through these things, why on earth she had to do it.' Does she feel sorry for me?'

It felt strange.

He was not accustomed to have feelings, he did not know what to do with them. Nothing, that occupied so far that part inside him, was better. Much better.

He knew where to stand then. No surprises.

It was a protective flatness to which he had been used for so long now.

These people had come though here to trouble him, to disturb this internal peace he had, starting to cover it with feelings.

How odd.

How obstructive.

He was annoyed.

'I suppose I can ask her politely not to repeat this.'

However they were kind people, and there is no way to fight kindness. It's a good weapon, very effective for those who use it.

Ching Lee finally realised that for the time being he had no other option than go along with it. But in doing so, he had to change, he had to make allowances for other things to enter him, and even this was unknown, the opportunity, he could not though find it an opportunity as such, to change things.

'But why to change things?'

Why he had to stop being what he has been for so long? It was OK, wasn't it? No problems, no fuss, about anything and anyone.

So, what was the point?

However, wouldn't it have been better to have some people around? Few at least, to speak to, perhaps to visit?

When he finished his meal and a generous portion of the cake, and moved it to his tiny fridge, he returned to his sitting room and went to search in his boxes.

He moved a few, and opened one full of paper birds and butterflies, and small animals.

Like a painter who draws with a pencil few caricatures on a piece of paper to rest from a painting, Ching Lee was making few paper toys, when there were no fans around to fix.

He took out three birds, two butterflies and a cow, placed them carefully on a smaller box, and wrote outside, 'for Abigail and the boys.' He had to present them nicely, so he folded the box on some colourful paper he found in the boxes too.

'They might like them, they are only paper though, but have pretty colours, and they can move them with the sticks I have fixed on them. There.'

He looked at his parcel, rushed quickly downstairs to leave it outside their door, this time not caring too much for the creaking staircase, and pleased that finally the matter was sorted out, went to bed.

5

Aaron had stayed home following the doctors orders for some days now, as his arm was not improving at all.
Ching Lee was worried for him.
He thought that for a guy like Aaron, full of energy and hard working, this must have been a blow. How could he survive?
Unemployment benefit, but was it enough? And what could have happened to him if for some reason could not work anymore?
He went down the staircase his head full of black thoughts about the future.
'Are you doing anything this Sunday, I mean tomorrow?'
The voice and question startled him.
'Good morning, I am sorry I got to you abruptly like this.'
Helen Morton was waiting for him on the doorstep of her flat.
Ching Lee looked at her, not knowing if he had heard well her question, and not being certain about this, he moved only his head in a greeting.
'The children were delighted with the toys, especially Abigail. I don't really know how to thank you for this, you should have not really go to this trouble to buy them toys.'
'I made them,' he said quietly, preferring that she would leave him alone.
'You made them! How wonderful, they were really charming. Well done to you.'
'Thank you, it's kind of you.'
'It's my Tom's birthday on Sunday. If you did not have anything better to do, we would like you to come to our home. There will be some children of course, and few friends.'
'Thank you again,' he was now certain that he had heard

well the invitation, 'I am working though at home on Sundays, I have to fix something for someone.'

'Oh' said Helen, 'it's a shame really, the children would have loved to show them how to move the toys.'

'That's not difficult, anyone can do it.'

Abigail pushed by her father, appeared on the opening of the door.

'We have to take her to the nursing home until we come back.'

'The nursing home?' Ching Lee was surprised.

'Well it's something like a special school and nursing home together, it's for children like her, they keep them occupied until the parents collect them again.'

'Ah' he said only, looking at their door as Abigail's eyes suddenly took an interest on him.

'Did you like the toys?' He dared now to look at the girl.

'You know Abigail, the gentleman here has done these toys all by himself, you should say thank you to him for his present,' Helen replied quickly on behalf of her daughter.

'Thank you,' said the girl like a whisper he just heard.

'It's my pleasure, if I will have some time I will make some more for you. Would you have liked that?'

'Perhaps' she said, and lost as she had found it, any interest for him again.

'Please come on Sunday' said Helen Morton, 'it will be nice to have you.'

'Thank you for your interest in me,' he said, and too shy to refuse again, but also making an effort to avoid her, 'perhaps' he said quietly.

'Oh, good. I am sure you will have lots of time to work until the afternoon.'

'Perhaps,' he said again, suddenly not finding any other word for the occasion.

'Thank you' said Helen.

'Good day' he nodded to them all and left.

He walked to the tube station with his mind full of this invitation that he had no intention, or wish to honour.

'Why they do not leave me in peace? I need lots of time to repair the fans, these are excellent pieces, very delicate, I have to be so careful, what am I supposed to do in their home, I know not their friends, and I do not want to be with children.'

He did not want any relationship with anyone, and yet Helen Morton has been kind, as well as pushy in her kindness, however was not intrusive, and that he was recognising. 'It would be unpleasant for them to refuse, perhaps not kind at all from my part, perhaps I could go for few minutes.'

He was debating this with himself even when he had reached the 'Dragon's Head' but still had not made up his mind whether he should go, or not tomorrow to Tom's party.

Mr Zhung looked at Mickie with his sharp, narrow, black eyes, as if he wanted to go through him.

'How do you know that this cook is good enough to fix the fans?' He asked, in his nasal, shrieking voice.

'I have good information about him,' said Mickie, petrified inside for his decision, 'why on earth I did not go to some proper antique repairers,' he thought, still quiet disturbed for what he had done, and fearing the worst from his boss in case anything had gone wrong with the damned things.

'What information?' Zhung still insisted.

'The man had studied a lot about this in Canton, in his time I mean, he was about to be the new curator at the museum in Nanking. I had good information I say about this, believe me boss I did not take them to him without asking my sources, I have good sources you know.'

'In Nanking you said?' Mr Zhung's eyes became even

69

more narrow now as they closed more than usual, he was watching Mickie very carefully, thinking that either this idiot of assistant he had was a big liar and a fool, something for which ever so often had no doubt at all, or really he had some correct information. 'What is he doing here then, being a cook?' He asked Mickie, as he was finding the whole matter a little stupid.

'I have asked him the same, but he has come here long time ago, in early seventies, that's what I was told, and when I asked him he said he could not find another job at the time. He is secretive, he does not like to speak, but he cooks well,' Mickie smiled on the thought of Ching Lee's food, 'we know that.'

'Yes,' agreed Mr Zhung, 'his dumplings are the best in that area. Early seventies you said?' He caressed thoughtfully his chin.

'Ah,' replied Mickie.

Mr Zhung watched the wall opposite his desk for some minutes without saying anything.

The other was watching him in apparent calmness but his heart was beating fast still on the decision he had taken deliberately.

'He will do them all right,' he reassured his boss, I got good information about this, trust me.'

Mr Zhung did not took his eyes from the wall, still stroking slowly his chin, 'trust you?' He asked appalled even on the thought, as a smile of disgust for the thought appeared in his lips,' we shall see,' he said only after sometime.

'You will pay for them as new if I am not satisfied.' He turned his sharp eyes

from the wall to the fat face of the other.

Mickie looked at him for few minutes, and decided to leave the room quietly, avoiding any further questions about his choice of fan repairer.

It was not his idea all that, and he hated the thought of

being forced to pay for the damned things, but he had little choice for anything else right now.

Mr Zhung stood there in his big desk with the brown leather top, and still for sometime was watching the wall opposite him, stroking his chin.

A miserable Sunday had come here to stay.

It had rained all night, and the continuous noise of the water falling on the glass of the windows, had left Ching Lee a soothing and calm feeling.

Beneath his duvet the silence of the night with the monotonous music of the rain drops, were forming for him some kind of protection from the outside world, a security he much needed and wanted.

The people, all the people, were very far away at moments like this. He was alone, only with the company of the elements, any elements, he wouldn't mind really. However he preferred this rain the repetitive, slow, continuous noise of the water that he loved.

There, in the warmth of his bed he was not afraid to think. Noises and smells, faces and scenes, could interchange without any fear from events, bitterness, and time.

Everything was clear during these hours.

The drops of the rain in the courtyard, the servants running around for their jobs, and him, raising occasionally his head from his long table, to watch the water as it was forming various pools on the tiles, leaking down from the leaves of the plants to the soil, which was drinking it, absorbing everything, and soaking into mud.

His friends when they were coming around to see him, caught by the rain on the road, swearing for the bad luck they had to walk on this weather, and his mother always eager, and quick to sent the servants fetching sweet meats, and other delicacies that the house usually had, to keep them satisfied, and calm.

Oh what a blessing it was to hear the rain at night, when

there was no need to go anywhere tomorrow, and life was in his hands, all of it, to decide what to do with it, away from everyone.

He turned around and pulled up the duvet higher around his head.

He couldn't care for sleep.

He had as much time as he wanted to sleep, when all would be over.

Grandfather used to tell him that.

'You will sleep very well then' he was smiling on top of his bed, 'get up now for school, then there would be plenty of time to sleep.'

'If it will continue raining tomorrow no one will go to the party though.'

The thought displeased him, as he did not really want the weather to spoil things for the children, they did not deserve that. Abigail would be alone again, with only the faces she knew everyday.

'Poor girl, whatever really has happened to her, how will she manage in life?'

Some lightning interrupted his thoughts, and he pulled the duvet even higher, hardly having out of it even one hair now from his head.

'That means that perhaps I have to go, I don't like that. All I wanted was to start with the fans, I will not go out, there is some food in the fridge, and most of the cake, I will be all right. However if no one else comes I have to go, there is no weather excuse for me, is there?'

Still debating the matter with himself, he fall asleep only to wake up at eight thirty in the morning.

He could not believe that he had slept so much, so unusual for him, it disturbed him as laziness was now taking over his time.

Then watching the water pouring down the windows without a break, he sat down nearly nine o'clock to have his tea, and decided to give another verdict for his late awakening. 'I was tired' reassured himself, 'very tired, I stand all bloody day, what you want me to be after all.'

Glad that the verdict had not been far from the truth, he cleared the table and started working on the fans.

The more he was now examining them, the more he was thinking that whoever possessed these, was really wealthy and with excellent knowledge for fans.

One, had a screen decorated with superb mother of pearl on the handle, it must have been perhaps inherited from some court attendant, concubine, or other, as the design on it was depicting scenes of immense beauty and delicacy, which three hundred years ago was only for the very high standing people in China.

'We would have loved to have these in the museum' he murmured to himself, handling the fan with such attentiveness and careful movement, as if it was ready to dissolve the next moment into pieces.

'What a beauty' he kept on advising himself, 'such work, what craftsmen we had then.'

By seven the Mortons had lost any hope to see anyone coming for the party, and Tom had resolved his anger by kicking some of his toys around the room, when a timid knock was heard on the door.

Everyone startled and looked quickly towards Helen that she had rushed to open.

Ching Lee showed up in the front room, wearing an old but still in good condition jacket and a clean blue shirt that he had just ironed for the occasion.

He was holding a box with some more of his paper toys, and now both the boys went around him, examining from the outside and for as much as they could see, its contents.

He gave them the box, 'it's for you Tom' said 'those in the blue bag inside the box, but the others are also for

73

Abigail, and your brother.'

He sat as quietly as he could at the edge of the sofa, and he tried to concentrate on the people around him, behaving in a manner that he thought it could have been more appropriate for the occasion. Little he knew on those things.

The social etiquette, especially of people in this country was alien and strange, however he thought that even if he had returned to China now, things like this would have not been much easier.

People change everywhere, time changes them, attitudes, conditions and situations, are turning life and society very quickly. Everyone wants new things, they invent them, or are imposed to them by others.

All habits and traditions, all manners and attitudes, last only for a small period of time, are flexible always, as humans are like that too.

In moments like this though little he cared for either, he thought only that he should have tried a little more, all those years ago, to accustom himself with what was happening around him, and approach people more. At least out of respect for this country that had given him some food, and a roof above his head, that had accepted him.

It was something.

It had been everything he had.

Abigail had fixed her eyes on the wall, opposite her chair, deciding not to move them from there, at least since he had come.

On the little time he knew her, she was showing no interest for anything.

'How do you understand a child like this?' Ching Lee asked himself with no hope though for reply.

It stuck on his mind, and despite the fact that he did not want to be seen as continuously watching her, he was doing so in every possible moment that his eyes were abandoning the examination of the carpet.

'Your cake was excellent,' he told finally Helen in an attempt for conversation. She beamed with joy.

'It was nothing really, I do it often for the children, but I am glad that you liked it.

'Is this rain going to last long?' Tom lost interest on the toys of his bag, and had moved to the window, as the time was passing and no other guests were showing up for the party.

The telephone had rang a couple of times, Helen that was rushing to it for news of other guests, was only coming back with disappointment to transfer their apologies, and as the time was passing, she at least was certain that the party had already finished.

'Why can't they come?' Tom was though still very upset for the absence of his friends, it's only rain.'

'I don't know dear' said his mother, looking at Elliott, her other son, who clumsily was trying to move a paper bird, from the lot that Ching Lee had again brought them today, 'perhaps later.'

'I doubt it' his father stretched hands and legs in his chair, watching Elliott too. 'Not like that idiot,' and bent to take the bird from Elliott's hands, 'you should separate the sticks first.'

The boy was watching him, so did the others, except Tom that stubbornly was keeping his place by the window.

Ching Lee thought that the father also had little idea on this and slowly got up and approached them.

'Let me show you,' he said.

'Oh do let him show you indeed' said Helen, moving her head on a small sign to Ching Lee, showing that she was in agreement with him that her husband too had little idea on the matter.

'Abigail,' said to her daughter, and approaching her

75

moved her wheelchair closer to the others, 'you should watch Mr Ching Lee how he is doing this, so you know how you play with these animals.'

The girl took her eyes from the wall that were stuck before, to the carpet, as her mother wheeled her close to the others, and showed no interest, or enthusiasm on what was going on around the table.

Ching Lee went closer to her, so she can see better than Elliott, and Berty, how to move the sticks, but still he attracted little attention from her.

'She has been like that since the accident' said Helen.

'That's enough,' Berty nearly shouted with anger, 'we discussed it, no more about it again.'

Helen shut up temporarily, and few minutes later whispered to Ching Lee's ear, 'I don't think it really matters to her a lot to hear about it, it's only my husband that gets upset you see.'

'You don't know that,' Berty had heard her, and was still angry.

'I will tell you about it another time,' Helen whispered again, determined to want to speak about her daughter's accident.

'Please Madame, you don't really have to do this,' pleaded Ching Lee, feeling now more at ease with these people, 'you must have hurt yourself already enough.'

'Helen, do call me Helen. Oh my dear, only I know what we have been through, better than all the others.'

Berty looked wildly at her.

'Fucking weather,' Tom said in despair from the window.

'Thomas!' His mother now shouted to him, 'I'll box your ears any minute now. 'You should not have them boxed on your birthday, but I'll swear I'll do it if I'll hear you say this word again.'

Tom shrunk quickly, with only Elliott now watching with interest Ching Lee's movement of the sticks.

76

The rain had not stopped even for a minute outside, with the water's noise so distinguished and loud, that many times was covering for the gaps of the small conversation of the humans inside.

Berty and Helen slowly left Elliott and Ching Lee alone with Abigail's total indifference, as they both had lost by now any interest on the event, which had prepared with so much eagerness, and which had collapsed without any apparent solution for its salvation.

They both went to seat at the once better looking sofa of their sitting room, drinking slowly their beer, and lost either of them, in their thoughts.

Berty's anger had evaporated as quickly as it had come, and Helen thought that at least they could manage to be less embarrassed to their only guest.

Ching Lee suddenly had become in this small, and rather pathetically decorated sitting room, the centre of any interest and movement.

Once, or twice turned towards Abigail, however she hardly noticed that, or show any interest, other than watching the immovable pile of the carpet.

Even Elliott was gradually now losing any interest he had shown before in moving the small, paper toys.

As sometimes all humans do things without registering them in the brain, not caring, rightly or wrongly, for their correctness, Ching Lee approached mechanically Abigail's chair and wheeled her slowly and carefully next to the table, so she could touch anything that was on it.

Pushing gently some plates with bites of food and some cakes aside, he paraded on the tablecloth his toys, the one after the other.

None of the parents were attracted to this, and stayed still with their thoughts in the sofa.

Abigail looked for a second the colourful parade of animals and then continued her eye walks on the pile of the carpet.

'Shall I show you how to make one?' Ching Lee addressed now both Elliott and the girl, 'it's quiet easy, all you need is some paper, and pieces of bamboo sticks, light wood can do too.'

Tom had stuck his nose on the glass of the window looking at the rain that was forming pools of water outside, and the occasional, distressed from the weather, passers by. 'I will undo this cow now and show you how you can do it again. Look Abigail,' he suddenly found himself addressing the girl only with ease, 'you can do it yourself, perhaps show the other children how to do it too.'

He stopped then for a minute, realising that his ease had perhaps being a little thoughtless, as he knew that Abigail could have hardly have any opportunity to show anything to other children.

Elliott went to join Tom at the window losing now completely any interest on animals on sticks, and Ching Lee saw himself as a clumsy, old clown, performing to a non interested, stiff and bored audience. It was useless and pathetic.

As everything was now falling into a void, where nothing and no one was attempting any movement, and if it was doing this, it was washed too into a more permanent nothingness, succeeded again by nothingness, he felt that his presence had become without any purpose, even that small one of a social visit.

He dismantled the cow from the sticks, on the belief that at least he could have finished this job, and prepared to see himself out.

'Happy birthday again Tom' he said to the boy, who did not even bothered to turn around and looked at him.

Berty and Helen suddenly realised that he was leaving when he was by the front door.

'Forgive us please for being such bad company,' said Helen quickly getting up from the sofa, 'please stay a little longer, I am sure that the children will be delighted, why you want to leave us so early?'

'I really need to do my work too,' he found himself almost whispering, 'I stayed enough, taking advantage of your kindness to invite me.'

'Nonsense' said Berty, stretching himself and waking briefly from his slumber, 'come and have a beer, you haven't even touch any food.'

'Thank you, I don't drink.'

'Awful' shouted Berty, clapping his hands, 'everyone should drink, what else is life there for?'

But all he wanted was to go back to his little flat, close firmly the door behind him, and forget about this.

At some stage earlier on he had even thought that he had a good day. He had been working all morning and part of the afternoon, before he came down here with Zhung's fans, and he had found the work exciting.

He was doing everything correctly in fixing them, and then he also had some rest with some other people. Life was slowly changing, and was finding this not too unpleasant. Of course the fans needed much more time, but he could have managed that.

He was even happy with the rain, and the fact that the other quests didn't turn up. He was not accustomed to deal with a lot of people, and years closed in the kitchen had helped a lot to it. So it was not at all a bad day.

'The cow is in pieces. How it will become a cow again?'

Like if a stone had fallen in the quietness of the room, Abigail's voice stirred a sudden alertness to attention.

Ching Lee turned from the door.

'The cow is in pieces,' said the girl again, pointing to the paper toy at the table and looking at him as he was standing by the door.

Helen made a movement as to get near her, but watching now Ching Lee approaching Abigail's wheelchair again, she thought of not finally doing it, as he would taken care of this.

Ching Lee went back to the table, and with quick movements put back together the pieces of paper and the sticks.

The cow revived intact.

He raised his eyes to look at the girl, Abigail stretched her hand to take the cow from him.

She hold it in her hands and tried to move it around as he had done, but she could not do it. In a sudden explosion she threw the little animal to the floor, and it went to hit the leg of a chair, folded now in two pieces.

Ching Lee bent to collect it, and despite the fact that the cow was now in a much poorer state, he put it slowly back together and gave it to her.

The tantrum of the girl though had not passed yet, and ready to throw it again to the floor, she was stopped quietly and decisively by the older man who took it back from her hands.

'Let me show you how you move it,' he said only.

He took the sticks and moved them up and down. Then, he placed them inside her hands, and holding them in his, demonstrated how she could repeat the movements he had shown her.

Helen was watching, Berty stretched himself once more, before taking from the small table by his side, another can of beer.

They did it once, twice, three, four times. Then, he left her hands alone, and slowly she did what he had taught her.

'Bravo, bravo,' said her mother in a rather bored mood, and returning to the sofa next to her husband,' well done, you see how good is Mr Ching Lee, you should thank him for showing this again to you.'

Abigail was moving now correctly the cow forwards and

backwards, again, and again, and again.

And when she had finished with the cow, Ching Lee gave her a bird, and a butterfly afterwards, and the little, green monkey.

He wheeled her now to the side the table, where most of the little paper toys were, so she can pick up those of the animals, or birds and butterflies she wanted, and in a moment that she had mastered to move them all, he even saw her smiling to him.

'Let me show you now how you can make these animals yourself.'

Abigail was watching his fingers folding and unfolding the paper, inserting the little sticks on its pleats. He took again her hands in his and directed the movements until by time afterwards she was capable of coping his movements correctly.

'I am hungry Mum,' Tom suddenly remembered to abandon his place by the window to the demands of his stomach.

'There is plenty of food on the table' Helen told him, 'go and help yourself,' and the boy without waiting for another permission, attacked the bites and cakes, followed by his brother, who thought that perhaps this was not a bad idea after all.

It was nothing too big, but Ching Lee was feeling content. It was something that was spreading now all over inside him, it was something like a pleasure, a satisfaction of being in use.

Not for any work, not for making the dumplings good and tasty, not for finishing a day, not for walking in a Sunday and the sun had shone all through the time of his stroll. Nothing like this.

Small as it was, it was not for his fans, for the first time.

He had left the Nortons nearly nine thirty in the evening, that was the longest time he had spent with English people, except the staff at the Immigration Office that is, or any people really all those years in this country, out of those at work of course.

Abigail had being dealing with his toys for the rest of the evening. He thought too that she had given him a little smile as he was leaving. Helen certainly was very pleased, she was laughing when she told him in a low voice, not to be heard, when he was at the door, 'it has been a very long time that we have seen her so pleased, nearly as before the accident. I think you did a lot of good to her, and I pray that she will keep this mood, at least for a while.' She turned to look at her daughter that behind her back, was still at the table, tackling the animals, the birds, and the butterflies in rows. 'It will occupy her for sometime, until she will give it up, but it was so good of you, thank you.'

'I thank you Mrs Morton for inviting me.' He found it suited him more to call her only that, 'I do not usually have any social life.'

'We thought of that, Berty and I, it's not good to abandon the people around you, and neighbours really should come first.'

'He wanted to ask her why she did not then invited the other ones to the party, but he thought that it was not his business to enquiry about that.'

He had left without saying much more, as in reality he hardly knew what more to say.

He went back to his flat, closing firmly the door behind him, something that he wanted to do for a long time now, but it was not for the same reasons as before.

Only to keep this small pleasure with him, the contentment, of having something of his liked, for longer, as longer as he could.

He went straight to the table at the sitting room and worked on Zhung's fans until he could not keep any more his eyes open.

'How shall I wake up on time tomorrow?' He questioned himself when he reached his bed, 'you will,' said a little voice he always carried inside, 'it's a habit now, you like it or not.'

The rain had not stopped at all. It was raining, and raining, and raining, with buckets of water coming down from the sky to the roofs of the houses, rolling even further to their windows and gutters. It carried on like that up until nearly two o'clock in the morning, but no one at the house was awake to witness it. No one except Abigail, who in the dim light of her room was still searching to find the toys that she had spread around her pillow.

She stretched her ear to listen to the falling water on the glass, however that was not there any more, as the rain finally tired from that continued journey of hers had finally stopped, and happy that none of her birds, and animals, and butterflies, would be wet as she would carry them with her to her school tomorrow, she too went to sleep.

6

Mr Zhung eyed Ching Lee from top to bottom.

Lao Ta, who was curiously watching the scene from behind the till, had a little satisfied smile in his thin lips, which was drawn there on the assumption that the dumplings had, yet again, performed well for his restaurant.

After all he had not done badly to employ the older man.

'He proved to be a good worker, and a quiet acceptable cook.

No salary complaints, no fuss, what more an employer could ask for these days? Above all no holidays, nearly never, apart from one, or two days in the year, that he had told him that could not work, as it had something to do with his relatives, wasn't it?'

With the smile still hanging, in his otherwise, dry face, Lao Ta continued to watch Mr Zhung talking to Ching Lee, whilst his thoughts were coming and going from his mind, all connected with this matter, and the pleasure he usually was granting to himself of being so right in his decisions.

'I have some more things for you to fix' Mr Zhung seized Ching Lee's reaction.

'More fans?' Asked politely the older man.

'Fans, yes, some of them are fans, but I also have some cases for fans, and other little ornaments.'

'What kind of ornaments?' Asked again Ching Lee, folding his hands behind his long apron.

'Nothing really too important, some statuettes, two or three mirrors, small, useless things, no one would like them these days, but you see they belonged to my dear mother.' He made a long pose. 'I was really her favourite child, she left everything to me, and I would like to think that where she is, at least she knows I am looking after them.'

'Kind of you' the cook told him, 'but I do not know if I am able to fix them. Are they badly damaged?'

'Some are, some not.'

'Ah,' said Mickie from the other side of the table, smiling without any purpose throughout the conversation.

'Mickie here,' said Mr Zhung, pointing to his assistant, 'will bring them to you one of these days. You did a very good job with the fans, yes good job,' and suddenly, as if he remembered that very minute, 'here' he said, and draw out of his pocket a black, long, thick wallet, 'that's for you,' and pulled a ten pound note offering it to the cook.

Lao Ta could not have been happier. Despite the fact that he could not hear their conversation, the gesture of Mr Zhung, who hardly ever tipped anyone, and so generously, was even one more proof that he had decided well for the cook.

Ching Lee pulled out of the pleats of his apron one of his hiding there hands, and pushed gently the bank note and the hand offering it, to their previous place.

'You paid me Mr Zhung,' he said, 'I thank you for your kindness, but tips are not welcomed. I do a job, I am paid for it.'

Lao Ta got upset now with what he was seeing.

'How dare he to refuse a kind tip, the old sod!' He thought.

Mr Zhungs's little eyes seized the older man again.

'Don't be so proud,' he told him, 'you have done a very good job.'

'Thank you again,' Ching Lee cut him a little annoyed for this scene in front of others.

Most of the customers were gone though, as it was nearly eleven, however Mickie and another man that Ching Lee did not know, were at Mr Zhung's table, and it was also Lao Ta, that he was watching everything, and some of the waiters. 'It's not necessary all this, I have done a job, you paid me for this,' and he got ready to leave him.

What it was really worse than anything else with this scene, he thought, was that his secret, his most well kept little hobby, or wasn't even that, was hardly kept for him any more. The waiters might have understood, or for what they could not understand ask Joy who could have not been of course more happy than obliging with all the informations.

'Where did you live back home?' Mr Zhung asked him very suddenly.

'Nanjiing,' the cook replied, getting now more nervous for the whole thing.

'You even called it with the old name,' observed thoughtfully Mr Zhung, 'it's called Nanking now, didn't you know that? Mickie here tells me that you have studied in the University. Is this right?'

Lao Ta dropped his mouth open.

Ching Lee hated right now everyone and everything in this room, above all Joy with his big mouth, but also Mickie, Zhung for being so nosy, Lao Ta watching, the waiters whispering.

For some seconds that he thought lasted much longer, his blood was buzzing in his ears, making the noise of a pump.

'Yes,' he nearly whispered, and trying again to compose himself, 'I am sorry Mr Zhung,' he said quickly, his face all red, 'I really need to attend now some things I have left in the kitchen, before I go. Give Mickie those things you mentioned, and I will do my best.'

Mr Zhung was not pleased, but something was telling him to be patient with this awkward person, at least for the time being. He padded him on the shoulder, and returned the bank note to his wallet. 'It will be time for everything,' advised himself, as Ching Lee was wishing them goodnight, and hurried to disappear behind the kitchen door.

Lao Ta was to observe that the scene had finished well.

The rain had stopped for some days now, and the cold was increasing its powerful grip on all.

The night was so cold and crisp, that when Ching Lee left the 'Dragon's Head' was even smelling on the air the snow that was coming.

'It won't be long now,' he told himself, and wrapped tighter in his coat.

Even at this area of the city were people were out in the streets until late, finishing a meal, or just walking and looking on the shops, now it seemed deserted, and easily could be accompanied by the noise of his own steps.

He felt uneasy about the meeting tonight with Mr Zhung. He did not like the man, neither did any of his entourage, however the small, shrewd cord inside him was advising that it would have not caused him harm to earn some more money. 'Sometimes Joy is right on certain things, the youth's mind is not always to be rejected. After all why I should be scared to let other people know what I was doing before, is not a crime, is it?'

Abigail was looking the snow with wide eyes, which were spreading their glance on the white cover, which was nearly everywhere outside this morning.

She had not seen any snow before, other than some in movies, and as she could hardly recognise the familiar shapes of the neighbourhood out of the window, she knew little of what to think about it.

She stroke the paper cow in her hands with confusion and amazement.

The snowflakes were succeeding one the other, falling with stable repetition, but gracefully, tantalising themselves in a dance like movement before reaching the ground, and mix with all the others there, part of the same, thick form, that was covering the road, the roofs of the houses, the cars, the dustbins, fences, window sills, and everything else that could reach, and be able to stand on.

'I do not think the children can go to school today,' Helen said in a rather depressing voice to Berty, 'at least not Abigail.'

'No one will,' he told her, 'damned weather, only I have to go, no matter what.'

Berty had changed lots of jobs in the last decade. He had been a cabby, electrician, plumber, lorry driver, school bus driver, bus conductor, traffic warden, gardener.

He knew little, or something of all these professions, been qualified in nothing really, other than watching football and shouting on the scores, or drinking beer.

He was not a bad man, but he rather had that frequent capacity people have here to change. It was not bad really, however sometimes it was not this, his only his fault, as Helen often used to see it so.

He was honest, no one could have taken that away from him, that's the truth, but Helen's view was the same with most of the women really, 'you hardly appreciate someone who carries a cross around.'

Years ago, in his youth, he had been in the apprentice of a carpenter, who thought that Berty had a real talent for the job, and many times, still now, was repairing furniture here and there, when he could have found that is, a job like that for him.

He was now with a removal company, and whether he liked it, or not, people moving house could hardly wait for the first falling snow to stop, in order to do it.

He kissed Abigail, gave a friendly kick to his sons, them too were wondering on the white scenes outside, and went to the front door.

Putting on his anorak turned to his wife, who together with

the boys was standing behind the sitting room window, entertaining the sombre thought of passing the day at home with the children.

Abigail would have liked to be wheeled nearer to the window to look outside better, but with her father gone, little she had the guts to ask her mother to do so.

Helen had never been harsh to her, not that, it was only something small that the girl could have never exactly identify, or be able to do so at her age, to give the correct word for it, something like a kind of antipathy, or some sort of shame for her, that was constantly occupying her mother during those years after the accident.

But even that could have not been described as definite, it was more of an absurd feeling that perhaps one was carrying, the other detecting, only that.

Elliott, bored with the same scene he was looking for sometime now outside the window, and securing, from what he had heard his mother and father saying earlier, that the school had to be forgotten for the day, he decided to go back to his room and read his new comic that had left there for some days now.

Passing Abigail's chair he thought that it would not have been a bad idea to get her closer to look at the snow, and he gave her chair a little push that put her nearer to the window.

She draw quietly the net curtain on one side to look better.

'Don't fuss with the net curtains Abigail,' shouted Helen, who turned around to check on her and Elliott, 'I broke my back to wash and iron them the other day for Tom's birthday, 'bloody people, no one bothered to turn up other that the Chinese, 'she told herself.

Elliott went near his sister again and pulled more the curtains apart for her to see outside.

'You wretched children,' retorted Helen, 'you are

making me mad,' however she stayed with Tom behind the window, without an attempt to correct Elliott's and Abigail's audacious move of the net.

Elliott winked to his sister and left to go to his room.

After Berty, he was the one who really cared for her more than the other two in the family.

He was a boy with lots of interests of his own, quieter than his brother, and a much better pupil than him. He was very young when his sister was run over by that car on the pavement, still holding Berty's hand, and despite the fact that the whole event had little registered on his mind, the pain in her for the years to follow, physical and other, was enough for him to increase the feelings for the girl.

In truth, the pain had registered with all of them, however each one had a different way to face it, and live with it.

Elliott knew nothing about distress, but he knew about sadness.

Abigail stayed there, behind the window, watching the falling snow in awe, as if these, small, white flakes could fill all the void, any void that her little life, and her condition were allowing her to have.

Helen abandoned them all after few minutes, only returning to Tom by the kitchen door, 'keep an eye to your sister' she advised, and wheel her back to her room when she wants to go there.'

Tom listened to his mother without turning his head from the window, looking outside for different reasons than Abigail, as this was still a lot more interesting than reading comics like his brother, or try to study a little the lessons he could have had today. All the fuss of the people passing outside, wrapped up, and some of them sliding on the white pavements, the cars splashing the white stuff everywhere, that was a small fun for his otherwise bored little life today.

It would have not mattered to him really to go to school, may be after all he would have preferred it than stay indoors, watching only outside.

Ching Lee left for work much later than he used to all the other time, using poorly the bad weather as an excuse, 'however even later than usual I will be there earlier than all the others' he thought, 'I doubt if anyone will bother to come for lunch, even worse for dinner today. May be we will close in the afternoon, we will see.'

The real reason of course was not the weather, this was certain, what really had kept him behind was the new work he had to do for Zhung.

He had spent hours last night examining and re examining the items that Mickie had handed him to fix. These had not been only very good, old items like the previous ones, these, all of them, the fans, their cases, the little jewellery boxes, the mirrors, had really the quality of museum pieces.

Ching Lee was certain about this, and for this reason more confused. Anything he had learned, anything he had seen, studied, or knew about it, was now confirming this to him.

'Were really the Zhung's such a wealthy and powerful family to have items of this quality, but also such rarity, as these wonderful, old pieces were, or something else was hidden behind them?'

From every aspect that Ching Lee was seeing this, his belief was that hardly Zhung's family could possess such high quality pieces. Without any exaggeration, which his coolness and long possessed objectivity in life had endowed him, he could say that these belonged either to emperors, or very important Mandarins, with whom, from what he knew at least from the gossip around, Zhung's family had nothing to do.

Once, or twice he had heard at 'The Dragon's Head' that

Zhung had made his money by himself, with dealings in trade, and no help from his family that were poor and left behind in China. Of course gossip is usually hardly a source of correct information, however Ching Lee's knowledge and instinct, this time at least were going along with it.

He had spent hours last night looking at those things, again, and again, and again, lost his sleep most of the night for this. He was not even certain if he could fix them all, it was fear all over him indicating that their rarity would have imposed impediments for him to do a job as good at least as like the other fans he had fixed for the man before.

It was a clear day, with the sun shining, and the white of the snow glittering under the light. The sharpness of the cold air was penetrating his body, but also had a refreshing effect on his troubled mind.

People were scarce and few to find at this time of the morning, despite the fact that at other times the roads on the way to the tube station would have been with lots of them ready to go to work.

The already thick layer of the snow was covering now any ugliness around the neighbourhood.

Should the artefacts of Zhung were not so deep into his mind, Ching Lee could have seen Abigail watching him from the drawn still net of their front room, and perhaps noticing her small hand waving to him.

However, neither the little girl, nor anything else was worth thinking today, little he knew too how he could have been able to concentrate on cooking, other than relying on the long habit of doing so.

It was very strange for him to see suddenly after all these years items of such quality, that he was only used to see those long, lost days, inside show cases.

'I have to find out, I do not trust the man, or any of the

characters he drags around with him. Could Mickie tell me anything? Better not to ask him, Joy is right, the fat idiot all he cares about is his belly and nothing else, he would have gone straight back to Zhung and tell him everything.'

The fans, their cases, the jewellery boxes, and the mirrors were still parading in front of his eyes even when the door of the carriage opened in front of him, and the few people waiting in the platform looked at him in a funny way, as he was standing there not even looking at the door, or knowing really what was that thing which had opened in front of him. He only woke up from his reverie when the first push came abruptly on his back, few others followed, and then he got in too and found a seat at a corner only to continue his thoughts from where they were left in the platform.

The few people at the carriage opened quickly the papers hiding their faces behind them with small interest for the news, but mostly faithful to the morning habit. Ching Lee researched the hard disk of his head, concentrating on any information that it could have provided him on what it was bothering him.

Joy did not turn up for work today, even when the kitchen clock showed nearly eleven thirty.

Only Lao Ta, and one of the waitresses had come.

When he entered the kitchen, his dark, little eyes nailed Ching Lee as he was bending over his pans.

'Where is your protégé?' He asked him in a voice that was heard in the kitchen loneliness as a poisonous hissing.

'Everybody is late today,' said the older man, 'don't you see the weather what's like? Very few trains ran.'

'I have come though,' he was not on the mood to accept anything.

'So have I,' Ching Lee told him, 'others perhaps have difficulties, besides he is not the only one who did not come.'

'He is not going to last here for long,' Lao Ta told him, closing the door behind him with noise, he did not like to be contradicted.

Ching Lee returned to his pans, totally indifferent today to any of Lao Ta's remarks, and caring little for the boy's future. He felt he had done as much as one like him could have done to help him. If someone does not want to take advantage for that at a young age, there isn't much more you can do, they pay for it in the years to come, late as it might have been then to put things right.

It was not before two in the afternoon that Mia, the waitress came to tell him that he was wanted on the phone.

Joy's voice sounded upset and broken.

'Father died, father died, he died this morning, I am in the hospital, he had a bad night, mother woke me up, we took a taxi, it was bloody snowing, hard to find one, he died a little while, here, I don't know what to do.'

Ching Lee looked at the wall behind the telephone, 'it needs to be decorated soon this damned place,' he thought, a little incapable to grasp what the boy's voice was saying, or letting registered inside with little interest. 'In which hospital are you?' He asked him after few minutes.

'Middlesex,' answered the boy.

'Wait a bit there,' said the older man, I will try to come as quickly as I can.

He returned to his kitchen looking around. Most of the food was prepared and hardly anyone came today, other than two men working nearby who bought some food to take away to work.

He went out to find Mia and returned with her to the kitchen, explaining her where everything was left to be kept warm.

'I don't think we will see any more customers,' she smiled stupidly, 'he should have let us go home today, but not him, awful man.'

Ching Lee left her going this time to find Lao Ta in the room marked as 'private.'

'Joy's father died this morning,' he told him quickly, and then reproachfully, 'you see this is why he did not come today. I have to go to the hospital now to help them, they have no one else. I have left everything ready in case someone else comes, Mia knows about it, I showed her.'

Lao Ta looked at him measuring his face for any lies, then he said wryly, 'go', and returned to some papers opened in front of him, only to raise his head again when the older man had reached the door, 'who's going to help you when you die then?' He said, looking at the other with a small, malicious laugh.

Ching Lee took that in, and closed the door behind him in a hurry to remove his apron and get ready to leave.

Lao Ta's last words had been registered unused now inside him, not knowing what to do with them, but deeply saved, however at that moment he did not know how often he would have to return to their chilly echo in the days to come.

Now the fans, the boxes, the mirrors had gone.

He was not sad, he had no feelings right now, 'perhaps later' he thought, responding to the indifference inside him for the news.

He was mostly confused, upset, one of those things that stir trouble in your chest, filling it with pangs that suddenly gather there.

He nearly slammed the front door of the 'Dragon's Head' behind him, knowing for certain that Lao Ta would be mad and swearing for both, him and Joy.

Lao Ta believed only in one thing, money. The more, the better, and the more you helped him to get them, the more he believed that you were the best of humans, and always you would stand at the pedestal of his esteem, provided you continued the supply.

Ching Lee stumbled on the snow in the pavement, and started looking for a taxi to go quickly to the hospital.

He checked his pockets for money, and glad he found two five pound notes.

Always scared for crime in the city, from all those things he could hear at the news, he hardly carried at any time with him more than that. Only just enough for a taxi to go back home in case of an emergency.

He went to a corner he believed that was a good spot to find a taxi, and stood there, his eyes scanning the roads, his head not much cleared of the cloud that the news had caused.

Suddenly the bulk of a black cab appeared at a distance, and Ching Lee threw both his arms up waving to the driver to stop.

Tom left his spot by the window when he thought that the entertainment provided by people struggling to walk on the snow, or cars splashing the stuff everywhere, was enough for this morning.

He went back to the room he was sharing with Elliott to find something better to occupy himself. However, he had forgotten Helen's instructions for Abigail.

She did not care though.

Staying there and watching out was not bad, everything was better than going back to the little hole, that her family used to call 'Abigail's room.'

It had a tiny window, nearly close to the ceiling, mostly a skylight, overlooking a back yard, which was a yard only by name, whilst it was no more than an empty space, filled with dustbins, and some dead, old plants.

She could not have seen anything from there, only the

flowery, little nets that her mother had hung.

Helen did not bother to come out of the kitchen to check again on the children, the silence of the house, even temporary, with all of them there, was enough of a blessing to challenge it.

'Do you see the snow?' Abigail turned to one of the paper birds she carried on her lap. 'Look outside, look at it. If I had let you fly, you would have been very cold now, yes? Wouldn't you?' She imitated her mother's protective voice.

She lifted it on her hands, and played with its sticks.

Suddenly, and on a movement she could have not anticipated, the paper unfolded, and the bird stopped to be a bird anymore.

Abigail tried to move her hands as the older man had showed her, however it was all lost, her skill, his wings, and the bird did not like to fly again.

Not a long time later, tears started coming down her cheeks, no fussy ones, but small, quiet, rolling quickly, perhaps out of fear not to be seen, following the one the other.

Not knowing a lot of the passing of time, or how long that it would take for the older man to come back, she fixed her eyes on the opening of the window, that the drown net was allowing to have, and started watching carefully the road.

However, the time was passing without Ching Lee's figure showing anywhere, and Abigail was fed up from waiting, running out of patience to see her bird fixed again.

On one of her usual, sudden tantrums, she tore off the coloured paper on her lap, smashed the sticks into small pieces, and dashed everything to the floor.

Helen decided to come out of the kitchen.

'Look there what you have done, why you destroyed now that nice thing? What's wrong again?'

Abigail sealed her lips, and turned again into one of her old, withdrawn moods.

Helen sighed, she had been used for long time on this, but she was decisive not to give in to the challenge.

She examined carefully the pieces to see if any of them could be saved, and when she satisfied herself that the bird was totally destroyed, she collected all the pieces and returned to the kitchen.

She had a strange way dealing with her daughter's case. No words.

Her belief was that sooner, or later things have to calm down, and Abigail should not use her condition to intimidate anyone. After all Helen had two more healthy children to look after.

When the others tried hard to get Abigail to speak, or calm down, she was reacting with silence, ignoring anything that perhaps might have helped the situation.

Even when hours were passing before Abigail say one word again, Helen refused to try soothing the girl.

She did love Abigail.

She knew that.

However, since the accident, her daughter's disability had thrown some kind of shame on her, as and if the child's condition had been a rare, and repulsive disease.

The girl fixed now her eyes on the worn out carpet, and they stayed there for long.

'Would like to have your lunch now?' Helen only shouted from the kitchen's door, as if and the food solution would have saved the situation, and getting again no reply she disappeared a little more content back to where she had come from. She thought that she had done everything she could.

With the boys occupying themselves happily enough in their room to come out and play with her, and Berty still out for a lot longer, Abigail had little hope of allowing herself to change attitude. If it would have been then a way to get her to behave, Helen had after all a good knowledge of that, she would have certainly tried it, but she knew that there was none.

Ching Lee found madame Luo and Joy sitting at a bench in the front hall of the hospital.

None of them was crying.

Madame Luo looked totally bewildered, and sad, and Joy, Ching Lee thought 'for the first time' had no intention of making fun, or mock anyone.

'I am sorry' he only found to tell them, 'and in such bad weather' as this would have anything to do in altering things.

Madame Luo raised her eyes to him, and Joy jumped up from his seat, when they both realised his presence.

The young man's eyes became confident now. No matter how he liked to tease the older man at the restaurant, he much more relied on him to deal with anything in life, than his father.

'Where?' Asked the older man and did not continue his phrase out of lack of courage.

'They took him away' said Joy quickly in full apprehension of what would have been the rest of the phrase. 'They told us only to send the undertakers when we are ready. I think they put father in a fridge.'

'They usually do' Ching Lee replied quietly.

Madame Luo allowed some tears to roll down whilst hearing this.

It seemed that the time, between finding out of her husband's end, and sitting at the front hall, had covered things with some incapacity in getting in everything that had happened.

The swift trafficking of nurses, doctors, other patients, relatives, friends, all the people who had filled the gap between night and day at the hospital corridors, was captivating for someone who little, if ever, had the opportunity to watch so many people around, and this had the benefit of distraction from the recent event.

But of course she knew everything.

Heart and mind though loved to escape at this time, more than other times, and she was pushed towards that direction, which was good for her right now.

It was an incredible task.

Sometimes she tried to fight it, as the occasional, 'never again' was floating to the surface, completely in order with what has happened.

Hu was not a great love in her life, not even a love in that sense.

'What did we know about love on those days? Who did really?'

Nothing.

But Hu was not a bad man, a little useless many times to do something better in life. Now she was coming to think of this, her memory rushing back to all those years they had together.

She had been harsh though, what chance he really had to do anything better.

Had they stayed in China perhaps this criticism could have been in place, but not here, not with what it had happened to them.

They were both children of warlords, wealthy, unskilled, always relying in the good fortunes of their parents, until everything came the upside down. Perhaps

Hu had been lucky after all to die in a hospital bed, and in older age.

What about Joy?

What would have happened to him in this strange land without his father.

It was Ching Lee of course, who had been very kind to them, the only friend they had, however he was old too, and hard working, little she knew of what could have happened to him too.

Madame Luo had been very busy with her thoughts indeed to allow time for tears, and death right now. Besides an old woman, in her late seventies always should have little to give to feelings. 'Many times they serve to nothing' she used to say, 'you deal with life any way it comes to you, that's the only correct way.'

Ching Lee sat next to them in the bench for a while to compose himself. Practical as always, he quickly thought of dealing with the next task, which was in this case Hu's funeral. Knowing the family for long he hardly believed that they would have any monies for this, or at least sufficient to cover everything, so other ways had to be found.

It would serve nothing to ask Lao Ta to pay in advance some of Joy's salaries for this, it would be really something out of the question.

He turned towards Joy, who sitting next to him on the bench, was already lost, counting the floor tiles.

'Have you thought of the funeral?' He asked close to his ear, out of fear not to upset madame Luo.

'No' said the boy, 'I don't know anything about it.'

'You have to, and quickly, they will not keep him in the fridge forever, this is only a hospital you know.'

'How much this thing cost?'

'It depends from what you want.'

'Father only had very little money kept for anything bad, I suppose we should use them now, but I don't think that were more than a hundred pounds.'

Ching Lee turned to look at him in despair. Little he had himself to help them.

'Did you give your mother a tea at least?'

'No' said Joy again.

'I thought of that' he wanted to tell him again how useless

101

he was, but restrained himself out of respect only for his mother.

He got up. 'I will get you some tea' he told her softly.

She gave him a little smile, looking also at her son for few minutes.

Ching Lee tried to orientate himself around, ready for the task. When he spotted the place, he went and asked for three teas counting also the coins he took out of his pocket.

'Do you want ordinary tea?' The girl at the canteen asked him.

He was confused a little. 'What other teas you have?' He asked politely.

'Green tea, herbal tea.

'Oh, oh' Ching Lee flushed with small joy on hearing this.

'Green tea please' he said almost glad.

The girl put the paper cups in a small tray, and she passed them to him.

He returned home late that evening, dragging his feet, and holding as closed around his body as he could his old coat. The night was freezing cold, and he was tired, bewildered and desperate.

Madame Luo and Joy, were pleased that he had stayed with them all this time, 'stupid boy, he could not have done a lot for his mother,' Ching Lee persuaded himself that he was needed there.

The man in charge of the hospital morgue was a kind and helpful soul. He and Joy explained with difficulty to him that the family would not have enough money for any burial, so he had phoned the hospital administration, and them then the local Council.

It was a long line of people involved, the one after the other, behind a telephone receiver that were deciding about Hu's body.

They have been kind to them, the older man and Joy

could hardly believe how everything had been sorted out. It was a huge relief to know at least that the Council would have helped to put some of the expenses for a decent funeral.

A couple of times Lao Ta's words to Ching Lee as he was leaving the restaurant this morning, were echoing back to his ears. They were more like the refrain of a song, repeated, repeated, that's all they could do, but he paid little attention. The funeral, and the arrangements for this were his prime concern right now.

There would have been time for everything else later.

He sat down in a chair at his front room. The flat was cold as the heating had been switched off sometime ago.

It was past his usual time of returning home.

At the table, covered with a light, like gauze, white cloth, were the fans, their cases, the jewellery boxes, and the mirrors, littering the simple wood with the rarity and excellence of their presence, all reminiscences of the better days they once had.

Ching Lee lift their cover and looked at them. Their beauty, even faded, the craftsmanship, the materials and colours, were but a most calming picture in this troublesome day.

'Zhung would have nothing of these,' he said in a tiring, like a whisper voice, 'nothing.'

Very softly, with utmost tenderness, he touched with his forefinger all of them, like if he was caressing the cheek of a baby, or the petals of the most beautiful rose.

'Nothing' he said again, passing his eyes over all of them, again and again, as and his glance was but a beam of light, which focused, illuminated, and shaded objects, 'nothing' he repeated.

Strangely perhaps, throughout the hours of the day that had gone, and despite its events, the thought for these items must have stayed intact inside him, looming around their provenance, studying over it, deciding.

The verdict had been given, coming out of his chest as a huge sigh with relief that he finally knew something about them, and that knowledge was also his deep feeling, which was hardly ever mistaken, but so often correct.

'Zhung could have never had these items in his family's heirlooms' he advised himself once more.

However little he knew of how had come to his possession, for that even his imagination tonight was unable to comprehend.

Ching Lee got up slowly to go to the bathroom, preparing himself for bed.

'It will not be an easy day tomorrow either,' he advised the face on the mirror above the washbasin, 'I can do with a little rest.'

7

It was a calm Sunday morning, with sunshine which provided that long wanted feeling to get away from the snow and the cold.

Not that the chill had improved a lot, but under the touch of the sun it was melting a little into a more acceptable and warmer presence.

With the heating inside the room, and the sunshine penetrating the tidy net curtains of Helen's front room, everything was getting more pleasant.

Abigail, for weeks now, had returned again into those sullen moods, forcing her mother to sought once more the assistance of the older man from upstairs.

There were times that even Helen's long tried methods of behaviour had no success with Abigail's temperament.

Ching Lee had given up his Sunday walking without hesitation, as the last few weeks tiredness and sadness had an overwhelming impact to his usual quiet and thoughtful composure.

Perhaps some time with the poor girl could have helped him too to get out of this.

Berty and the boys took advantage of the sunshine and went to see a football match.

Helen stretched her feet watching television, only occasionally looking towards the table where Ching Lee had spread now out all his coloured papers, glue, sticks, and scissors for Abigail.

The girl had looked at him strangely this morning, he thought he had detected some feeling of betrayal, for the reason of which he had no idea.

Even nearly half an hour later, her attention to him making some new paper toys for her, had resulted to nothing.

Ching Lee wheeled her chair as close to the table as

possible, and with simple movements working on the pieces of paper he had brought for her, started showing the girl how she too could make some shapes of animals and flowers.

'You are very patient' Helen said, looking towards the table for a second.

'Abigail here is a very nice girl' said Ching Lee, watching with a kind smile the girl's face, as it was still dropped on her chest, refusing to raise it and watch his work. 'She deserves patience,' the man continued, 'but she will learn soon to make them herself, and then she will not need me to show her anything, isn't that so Abigail?' He got no reply again as a new yellow bird was ready in front of her chair, for her to play.

'Shall we do a butterfly now?' He asked once more.

Abigail refused to look at him, or open her mouth to give any noise.

'Mr Ching Lee had asked you something, why don't you reply to him?' Helen was remembering again the rules of politeness, as little as she really cared for her daughter to keep them.

Ching Lee found difficult to place Helen somewhere inside him. He hardly believed that she was dedicated to the girl, and then again her kindness to him and interest, her general good attitude to the other people in the house, were rather placing her to the side of good people, or at least those he considered to be good to him.

'Perhaps the pain makes people to seem harder than they really are, he had thought. 'No one is perfect, we all have our blemishes to show.'

'You did not come to save my bird.' Abigail's little voice came as a whisper from her head that she had dropped to her lap, and startled the older man.

'Which day?' He asked her, embarrassed that he had not manage to find out before about this.

'Which day Abigail? I know nothing that you lost one of your birds.'

'The day with the falling snow,' she replied to him quietly, and still keeping her head down. 'And you did not reply to me when I waved you my hand from the window.'

Ching Lee made a painful grimace as he understood that he had been the main reason for her recent sullen mood. 'I am so terribly sorry,' he told her, 'however I had a very serious problem, and I was distressed and unhappy too. You see, I also lost a friend,' he stopped.

'What happened?' Helen suddenly was attracted to the conversation, as one of her ears had been free from the telly.

'Oh, it's an old story,' said the man. 'You see, all those years ago that I came from China, I met a young family who had fled the country the same time as me. The man was my only friend, the only one I could speak to sometimes for things other people could not understand. He was nothing exceptional, but not a bad man.'

Abigail stole a look or two of Ching Lee's face, her antenna of loneliness already collecting a message of sadness there too.

'What happened to him?' Helen's curiosity left the programme she was watching on the television entirely.

'He died,' he said.

'Oh, I am sorry for you, 'said Helen when finally found what had happened lost any interest to the story and returned to her television programme.

'Died?' Abigail's voice increased slowly its volume.

'Yes,' he replied, 'like your bird too.'

'Could you not have fixed him then?'

'Don't say nonsense child. Humans are not things to fix.' Her mother was rather annoyed that the conversation of her daughter with the older man yet again had distracted her from her programme.

Ching Lee smiled.

'No' he said, 'I could not fix him at all.'

Two inquisitive eyes searched his face with interest. When they discovered there something of the same pain that they had too, slowly returned back to the coloured paper for support.

As the hands of the older man continued to fold it to the shape of a butterfly, Abigail's trust for him returned in happy, small intervals of a broken smile.

It was good to have him.

Now it was everything all right again.

She stretched her hand to the table and took one of the coloured papers there, then watching very carefully the older man folding it, she too repeated his movements in a clumsy but full of energy, joyful way.

Whenever she showed signs that she had stuck with it, Ching Lee helped her quietly.

Soon, they both look absorbed in this tedious but pleasing for both occupation of their hands, which boring as it might been looking, was releasing time and sadness in a useful way.

Silence was now resting in the room with only the presenter's voice on Helen's TV programme prattling in that space.

The older man had left the girl to crease, tear, throw away the pieces of paper that she could not fold correctly, and for the first time this waste of his few pounds gave him joy.

He really could not explain this very well, but it was like plunging into a slumber of bliss, thoughtless of all efforts, forgetful of all the time he had spent in earning those few pounds that Abigail now was wasting away, other times with a smile, and others with her usual, little temper.

'Do you know how it's called this that we are doing right now?' Ching Lee asked her with his small, quiet smile.

'No 'she replied, and raised her head to look at him.
'Origami.'
'Origami,' Abigail repeated correctly after him
'Origami?' Asked Helen, whose one ear was always dedicated to them, despite pretending that she was watching the telly.'What is this? Chinese I think.'
'No ma'am' said the older man, 'it's Japanese. You see they took lots of things from us and gave them other names afterwards.'
'You discovered this too?' Helen asked again vaguely, as she hardly cared, or have understood what really 'origami' meant.
'We discovered the paper,' Ching Lee replied seriously, our Buddhist monks took it to Japan in the 6th century.'
'Oh' said Helen, 'you know so many things Mr Ching Lee,' and decided at that point to stop the questions and return to her programme, as she could hardly give a toss for any of this.
He paid no attention to her remark, but he was carefully watching Abigail folding a creased, green paper again and again, and again, until after sometime the shape of a small butterfly appeared battered and shaken, but well shaped from her hands.
'Well done! Well done indeed!' He told her as his face beamed with joy watching the green butterfly making her small, hazardous fly in the hands of his pupil.
Abigail got quickly his contagious joy and looking at her achievement, smiled to the older man in a broad, happy smile.
Nothing could spoil this for either of them now. Not Helen's bored presence, or the TV presenter's snobbish accent and prattling with nonsense voice, not even the fact that the sun was long gone outside and darkness swiftly was replacing him on the windows.
None of these had any involvement, or could create any

interruption to these small, blissful humans.

Abigail's happiness was filling for the first time the cold and lonely heart of this old, Chinese man with joy.

How many years he had not really felt that.

All that passing of time that he could hardly knew its existence, the existence of this feeling to be happy with another human being. Even on those long gone days that he was debating the existence of happiness with himself. What was it really? Was it something big, or small, something that was capable to cover everything inside? And always the same reply was coming back. Nothing was big, nothing is really big in life, all are but small moments, they last few seconds, few minutes, that's all and keep you content, or not.

Happiness then was nothing more than capturing those small, quiet moments, let them register inside, and enhance your life with their warmth, no more, no less.

But this joy, this unexpected small bliss, to make this child smile, was indeed one of those moments, the feelings from which he had long forgotten.

In the other days it was good to fill the time, all the time, as this was helping him not to think, as thinking was the worst occupation of his mind. Then, all his ghosts were coming back, again, and again, and again, to stay and torture him, and that petrified him.

The suppression of scenes, that even faded were still painful, the everyday empty routine of repeating the same things in the hope that in their repetition no sadness, or pain will return.

All that was gone.

No pain occupied anything inside him at this moment, no fear for his lonely existence, no bitterness for all those things that were inflicted upon him.

Abigail, in a small delirium of joy was still cutting the air with her green butterfly in hand, and him, the old

Chinese, that bothered no one, and no one was bothered with him, stood there watching her proud and pleased as no member of her own family ever was.

He had achieved something.

He had made Abigail happy.

He had taught something someone, who was depending upon him and his colourful, folded paper shapes for joy.

When Abigail got tired to move her arm up and down in the air, she landed the butterfly with care on the table.

'What else are we going to do now?' She asked Ching Lee, as her brown eyes had enlarged from joy and anticipation for more fun, forming two little lights that were focusing on his face.

'I will teach you how to make paper fans,' he told her, and took a red paper in his hands.

'Ah, how nice Abigail,' Helen jumped again into their world without any extra thought, 'you see how good is Mr Ching Lee to you, and you have not yet thanked him.'

'It's nothing important,' the older man replied, 'I don't really do anything.'

'You should not say this, you have already done so many things for Abigail.'

'Please, please,' Ching Lee tried to stop her, detecting that the girl's enthusiasm was falling quickly from her mother's intervention.

'No, no,' insisted Helen, 'children should learn to recognise what you offer them and respect it.' Helen was now on strict motherhood mood.

'My grandfather used to say that,' the older man told her smiling.

'He must have been a wise man.' Helen grasped the opportunity to use a word that she would have liked to be attributed to her too. 'How right he was indeed.'

Ching Lee smiled again and continued to fold the red paper in the shape of a small fan. It was getting dark when he left the Morton's that Sunday afternoon.

Even Berty and the boys were pleased to see Abigail in such good mood when they returned.

'You performed miracles,' Helen put her hand on his shoulder at the front door, 'I can't remember how long ago it was that I have seen her like that.'

'She needs someone to cheer her up, 'he told her quietly, 'besides the joy is all mine, it's very good to see her pleased.'

'You are good mate,' Berty followed them unnoticed.

Ching Lee turned to him, 'I hope the match was good' he asked politely.

'Not bad,' said Berty, 'the lads liked it though. It's something for them.'

'Good, good 'remarked the older man and left them trying to avoid further pointless conversation.

When he returned to his small flat and closed the door behind him, Ching Lee had that rare feeling filling his heart that this really had been a very good day.

Abigail until the time that her mother put her to bed, was doing nothing more than folding the remnants of the paper Ching Lee had left behind and they were now scattered in the dining table, in various strange shapes. As her hands were getting more and more into it, the shapes were slowly taken some known forms, until finally a fan, a bird, and a hen, managed to come out ready to circulate in life in a shaken but not bad condition.

Her room was now full of them, the latest ones coming to add on the collection that the older man had made for her.

They were around her pillow, stuck on her duvet, even filling her little hands, until sleep, quiet and joyful came to claim her that night.

'She had a good day,' said Helen to Berty as he showed his face on Abigail's door. 'That Chinese man is getting along with her very well, as and the rest of us do not exist. All these days she was in a bad mood, and then he changed everything.'

'He seems a decent kind of fellow,' said Berty, 'he doesn't talk much to find out more about him, but I think he is OK.'

'I always keep an eye.'

'I don't think really that you should.'

'Better safe than sorry.'

'Come on, you see problems everywhere Helen, he is all right, simply he gives her time and she is attracted from those colourful shapes he does for her. Perhaps we should give her more time, or see on what she is interested.'

'Nonsense, we have given her all our time. How old you reckon he is?' Helen closed Abigail's door behind her.

'I don't know, hard to say with these people, they all look alike.'

His wife smiled.

'I think he must be well in his seventies, 'she replied her question, 'god only knows what made him to come here.'

'Prosperity,' Berty laughed heartily now, 'he has it hasn't he? He cooks all bloody day and returns to Price's rotten hole.'

'It's not that rotten,' said Helen, not to include themselves in the characterisation, 'it simply needs some work done to it.'

'Yeah, yeah' Berty continued laughing.

'Perhaps we should find a bit more about him.'

'Why? Is there any reason for that? He is all right, after all it was only you that started being friendly, why poking now into his life? Leave the poor man alone.'

'But he started been close to Abigail.'

'So? He is not harming her, on the contrary, he is the only one who put a smile to her face, which obviously none

of us achieved for the last whole week. Leave him alone.'
Helen did not continue the conversation, she cared little
though for the advise her husband had given her, already
her mind trying to find ways to collect more information
for the older man. Deep down a small feeling of jealousy
had started lurking inside her for Ching Lee, as he
had managed what all were finding difficult to achieve,
Abigail's interest for something and good moods.
Ching Lee went straight into his front room and sat at the
table.
The fans, their cases, the little mirrors, and the jewellery
boxes, were parading in an orderly fashion wrapped tidily
in bubble plastic sheets and ready to be delivered to
Mickie tomorrow morning.
 He felt a pang in his chest that all those precious and
so wonderful for him things, the pinnacle of his country's
craftsmanship for this sort of work, had to return to
someone like Zhung.
'I know not a lot about him, so I shouldn't think bad of him,
he pays me after all good money, but..' his consultation
to himself could not be complete without his gut feeling
for the man, which was not a good one. 'I should not be
prejudiced, nonsense.'
He stopped and looked again on those plastic shapes in
front of him with a sad smile.
However, it had been a good day today, he should not
have any complaints about it, or spoil it in anyway, only
that it was difficult not to miss them.
He stood there, his slim body immobile, fixing his eyes on
those things on his table and with a dry smile to his lips,
got lost in another world that his thoughts had transferred
him.
It was a time that he had no fear of remembering, and
closed inside his small space, warm and secure for the
time being, content that in this day he had been lucky

enough to be a human in its full meaning, the ghosts could be easily released from their locked cases and allowed to come around him.

He was full of everything right now. Bitterness, anger, disappointment, loneliness, sadness, despair.

All that dance of feelings had no purpose of course other than opening the door were everything was kept tightly closed, its exodus for limited time had only the purpose of some relief from all that weight gathered there.

The night was falling very quickly, and it was nearly eleven o'clock when Ching Lee suddenly sent his ghosts back to their cases again and picked up on the world around him. He rearranged the items on the table closer the one to the other, and went to retrieve from his kitchen a plastic bag, big enough and good enough, to place everything inside, ready for Mickie.

It was and as if all those, correct for him, tidy acts were part of a procedure essential for his small life. Then only he had no more to complain for, and the quietness that all those regulations were bringing were a reassurance for the passing of a good day.

However, when all those had been performed and for the last time the fans, their cases, the jewellery boxes, and the small mirrors, were unwrapped in order to be wrapped again in seconds, even more tidily this time, the same agonising thought about their provenance returned to annoy him.

Looking at them again, examining the decorations, the materials used, and the quality of the work on them, Ching Lee confirmed to himself that these items were of such rarity, that only a state's museum, or an extremely knowledgeable and wealthy collector could possess, and Zhung was neither.

With great care, fondness and sadness, he wrapped the pieces of the bubbled plastic sheets around them for a last time and secured them with a tape.

Everything now was placed in the bag he had selected to be worthy for these treasures, and ready to be taken tomorrow to the restaurant.

He had asked Mickie for six hundred pounds, a price which was to his surprise accepted, and that he thought now that was very small as he was reassessing how much they were worth, and the extremely difficult and delicate work he had done on them, repairing them.

At the same time he felt a pain for some little voice inside him that consistently was calling him a traitor.

It was a voice he hated to listen to but that it was always finding a way to come out. What should he have done then?

How could he had his fears confirmed?

Where could he had gone and ask, report about it?

Report what really?

All he had were but his assumptions, based on old knowledge. And what if he was wrong?

What if indeed Zhung had inherited these items?

Why was him that was a traitor?

It was his job, it would have been his job to fix, or ask for other craftsmen to fix these items, which could have been shown in their museum in Nanking, if everything had not gone so badly wrong. Now he knew, and he was going to get money for fixing them as and if he was but a simple employee, a craftsman only like the others, was it right after all?

He went to the window and draw a corner of the curtain. The night was deep but not very dark, as some stars and a very anaemic moon were trying to light it a bit. There was no one out in the street, and the windows of the houses were all looking like closed eyes, deep in sleep.

'Perhaps I should do the same,' Ching Lee advised himself, 'I am but an old fool and nothing else.'

8

Mickie looked at the wall, pressing his nails in his palms as strongly as he could, but not reacting to the pain he was inflicting himself. Drops of sweat were covering his forehead, but otherwise his usual, idiotic smile, was still hanging in his big mouth.

Mr Zhung opened slowly the bubbled plastic sheets that were covering the various items, left by Mickie, the one next to the other, on his desk.

He discarded the wrapping, and hold the small mirror, decorated all around with small stones and mother of pearl, in his hands. Folding both his hands around its handle raised it more towards the light that, with difficulty was trying to get in from the windows.

'How much did you say you paid him?' He asked his assistant.

'Six hundred. It was a lot of work he told me, I think he was not wrong on that, they were not in a good state. I tried for five hundred, he refused to do them, I really tried many times.'

Mr Zhung looked at him without any expression in his dark eyes. He took another of the items and unwrapped it slowly.

Mickie realised that his nails, long and hard as they were, were cutting the skin in his palms more and more, and opening his hands now, changed their position by keeping them around the arms of his chair.

Zhung took finally out of its wrapping the second item, and examined it like the mirror, with great care.

It was a cockade fan, which was opening and closing around the main stick, all round in shape. He looked at the magnificent drawings of birds and flowers in the paper, the pierced handle, then he folded and unfolded it slowly and carefully, two or three times before letting it to rest on his desk.

The one after the other all the items were unwrapped and examined in a long, quiet, and extremely careful ceremony of gestures, keen and concentrated eyes, in silence.

Mickie had lost by now any track of time. Every single bad word he knew, was repeated inside him more than once to keep him in line with Zhung's examination. He knew well that Zhung would not say a word if he did not liked what he saw, however his punishment would be long and harsh, not possible to avoid. It had been a long experience for him. That was why despite the very cold weather, the heat inside the room and his agony for the outcome of the examination were causing him a flush, which had turned his entire face red, and sweat was running down his back uncontrollably. His shirt sticking between his jacket and his body, was by now wet like in a very hot summer's day.

'It's a brilliant job.' Said Mr Zhung after some time that Mickie thought that it was ages. 'Well done, we will give him the other things too. Go and get them now. But wrap these again, before you do anything else.'

The same way as he had unwrapped them before, he tried now to fold again every single thing into its bubbled sheets, in careful, slow movements.

Mr Zhung looked at Mickie with some disdain,"wrap these well," he ordered him, showing the plastic which was creased badly around one of the fans, realising also that the job was not easy for him," and be very careful," Mickie eased his hands from the plastic sheets,"Ah," he said with a smile and dedicated himself to do what he was told with obedience and relief.

"Be gentle with the older man," he scratched his chin now Zhung," it seems he is who they told you, he has quality. Give him whatever he asks."

" But," Mickie was surprised at the change of mood,"you have told me.."

"Forget that," Mr Zhung cut him quickly with an icy tone to his voice,"he did a good job, you don't find others like him here that know so well how to deal with things of this kind, there aren't any, I know that better, I have been at this game for a long time not to understand a good craftsman." Mickie moved only his head," do you understand what I am saying?" Mr Zhung's tone was now angry.

"Ah," Mickie repeated.

" I doubt it," said Mr Zhung to himself." You will answer to me if this doesn't go well," he got up abruptly from his desk to give an end to the conversation.

Then, he returned again near Mickie's chair, where the other was still standing with his mouth half opened, he bend towards him nearly hissing on top of him,"do you understand?" He repeated, moving around and even closer. Mickie sat quietly to his chair, tightening his grip again to its arms.

As Mr Zhung was bending on top of him small drops of saliva reached his forehead.

" Yes boss" he said.

Mr Zhung left Mickie and the room in a fast pace, banging the door behind him, only to appear again two minutes afterwards.

"Get those other fans to him," ordered his assistant, in a quieter voice now.

"I had that in mind, as you said before, but I want to ask him first. He likes to be asked you know."

"Good, do it," said Mr Zhung and left again the room, leaving this time the door open.

Mickie was scared to feel any relief right now, but he started wrapping the items again, with as much care as his clumsy movements were allowing him, in Ching Lee's

119

same wrapping sheets.

He had not even the courage to swear inside him as he did before, and as he used to do so often after Mr Zhung's orders. Everything was dressed in a flat fear inside.

He knew well that it would take Zhung few moments to send him out of work and this house.

He thought that although he might have survived that, as he always believed more for himself than others who knew him, but things, he was certain on this, would have not been as comfortable then, and that he did not liked.

He was coming really from the gutter and the last thing he wanted was to end up there again.

When he finished, he went out in search of Mr Zhung to ask for further instructions, in case he wanted to add some more items to the next assignment for Ching Lee.

Mr Zhung was living at a large house in North London with three floors and a nicely cared for garden.

There were a couple of other people visiting, in and out, on several days of the week, but Mr Zhung, Mickie, and the maid Sue, were the only permanent residents.

Mickie and Sue were occupying the two bedrooms under the loft, which, like the basement of the house, was full of all sorts of old items.

Only Mr Zhung and Mickie were coming here though, Sue's duties were usually keeping her busy on the other floors.

These rooms were locked up at all times, and Mickie carried out any basic cleaning in them when Sue had her time off.

She was a plump, short young woman in her mid twenties from Weymouth.

Looking at her, and especially at her substantial backside, one could not but think of a little, fleshy hen that walks moving slowly the one thigh after the other to attract a male.

There were times that Mickie fancied her a lot, however he knew that she was occasionally keeping company with Mr Zhung, especially on some cold winter nights when nothing else better was around, so he did never dare ask.

Berty sent a sideways look to Abigail as she was watching with interest outside the window of the car. She was quiet as usual, but she was clutching in her lap a paper bag full of her new toys from Ching Lee. He hardly remembered her before looking outside the car's window, only occasionally concentrating her attention, if any then, at the fabric of the skirt she was wearing, around her little lap.

"Do you like them?" Berty smiled lightly to his daughter pointing with his eyes at the toys,"he is good the old chap, isn't he?" He continued, as she did not reply to him.

Abigail turned her head towards him only after few minutes had passed as if she had only now heard his question, or as even she was still thinking what to reply. So far, she had kept sitting quietly next to her father in the car, in their usual morning drive to her school.

" I know now how to make up some of them myself," she told Berty after a very long pause and when he was least expecting a reply, and she drew out of the bag the yellow bird, and a green cow.

"What, you did those two all by yourself?" Berty wondered, being also now genuinely surprised and pleased.

He always loved his daughter, however her accident in his presence put him into some kind of a strong debt towards her too, increasing always his affections.

In very, many ways Berty felt guilty. This was really and clearly the deepest feeling for Abigail. Guilty that he had not been able to protect her, as he should. Helen was always quick to remind him that on most of the times that any discussion was looming between the two of them about Abigail's future. Their daughter's condition had been a thorn that had torn them apart, perhaps even more than their usual bad financial state had achieved.

If his wife's goal was to put that guilt to him for future use and responsibility, she had certainly achieved it.

" Yes," Abigail replied,"and Mr Ching Lee has also taught me to make some fans too, but I have not tried one yet, I will though, I liked those he made for me."

"Great love," said Berty,"that's quiet good."

Abigail smiled to him, and for the first time he detected a small light in her eyes, where usually a flat indifference for anything, resided before.

"Is it going to snow again Dad?" Abigail asked him after some time.

"Oh, I don't know love, perhaps yes, perhaps not, however is still winter you know, winter is not a good season, it's cold, it rains, it snows. Why?" He added looking at her,"you don't like the snow, do you? No one does really," Berty replied for himself mostly now.

"No," said Abigail," no, I like it, I love it. I like to see the white flakes dancing on to the window."

"Then, it might snow again, perhaps yes, it will," said Berty.

Abigail gave her father a broad smile, which was reciprocated as Berty also stretched his hand from the gear he was holding, to squeeze her little fingers clasping the paper toys in her lap.

They continued their road to school without any other interruption, pleased both that in their poor capacity of one giving, and the other taking, strength, courage, feelings, guilt, harshness, at least, they had managed to achieve those few moments of contentment and small happiness. Only when they had finally reached the school, and Berty was getting ready to get out of the car, Abigail's little hand touched again his arm.

"Dad," she asked thoughtfully, if not without bitterness in her voice.

"Yes love."

"Do I have to go to this school?"

Berty sat back to his seat.

"What do you mean?" He tried to win time in order to understand her question,"all children of your age have to go to school to learn something. It's good for your future." He stopped there abruptly, realising how stupid the last words were sounding in the emptiness of the small space. He hit the wheel with his hands. He could not cope with difficulties, he was a simple man, he knew only few concrete things in life, like work, house, food, transport, family, and Abigail's question had nothing to do with it.

"I mean this school," the girl continued, just to make things a little worse than what they already were."I don't like these children, they are strange."

Berty hit the wheel again and looked vaguely at the dashboard,"I know love," he said after few minutes had passed, during which Abigail's look was continuously falling to his face,"I really do," as suddenly decided to express his gut feeling for what somewhere inside him shared with her regarding the kind of children the school had gathered.

Abigail squeezed her father's arm again,"will you take me away from it then?"

He looked at her face, pale, thin, with two eyes that something small was flickering there with hope.

" I will think of it" he said after some minutes,"I will think of it and speak with yours teachers, and your mother."

The fact that he would have asked first the teachers and then Helen gave the girl some small reassurance that Helen's influence would have not been very important this time, and that Berty was perhaps a bit serious with his promise.

She waited patiently for her father to get her out of the car, and Berty grasped quickly the opportunity of having no more questions to reply so he rushed to do his usual task to assemble the wheel chair.

Ching Lee was looking Mickie as if the latter was coming from another world.

"Where did you find these?" He asked, pointing nearly with anger at the items inside the open package left on the kitchen table.

"Mr Zhung wants you to fix them," Mickie repeated what he had just told again the older man, totally indifferent to the other's annoyed expression.

"I heard that, but this is not what I have asked you. Where did you find them? Or, better where your boss found them?" He separated now the words in his last phrase, which one by one dropped in the quiet, at this time, restaurant kitchen, with some strength of their own.

"Mr Zhung had them in the basement," Mickie replied truthfully, only to add later,"why you care, that's only a job for you, mind your own business."

Ching Lee raised his eyes to him with more anger than before, thinking now more than any other time, how right Joy was about this idiot.

"I could have sent you and your boss's items out of here," he really hissed to Mickie. Then, completely ignoring him,"Mr Zhung had them in the basement," he repeated, having his last hope to try and swallow this information the assistant had provided.

He fixed his eyes again in the package, the two fans in it becoming now more the main element of his concentration.

He took the one out, with religiously slow movements, and examining it carefully,"I hope I am wrong," he murmured to himself,"oh I do hope I am wrong."

Mickie was looking, he could hardly understand what the

other one meant, or why he was so much insisting on the provenance of the fans. Everything was becoming more and more complicated for him.

Ching Lee ignored him and concentrated again with the items for the rest twenty minutes.

He was raising them to the light, examining their sticks carefully, the material of the leaf. Then, he was leaving them carefully on the table again, looking them from where he was standing, afterwards stepping back, and then closer to them again.

"Why do you do all that?" Mickie could not restrain himself from asking, thinking at the same time that perhaps the old lunatic was doing all that in order to extract more money from his boss.

He ignored him again, giving no reply to his question.

Ten minutes afterwards the fat assistant started becoming red in the face, and increasingly impatient.

"Now, what do you think you are doing? Could you let me know? I have other business to attend, you know that, I have no extra time to kill sitting here and waiting for you to finish your tricks.'

The older man did not bother again, either to look at him, or reply, his main concentration still devoted to the fans he had laid open on the white tea towel on the kitchen's table.

"Will you do them?" Mickie increased his tone too to match his impatience, adding anger now to his voice.

"I will keep them and think of it," Ching Lee replied suddenly, very calmly,"I need to study the way of repairing them," he added finally looking at Mickie's face with shrewdness.

"Why the hell it took you so long to say that?" Mickie was finally relieved, but upset with the older man's attitude."What was all that about where Mr Zhung found them, don't you really care that he likes you to do this job and get some money after all, that's stupid." Mickie was getting out of his system what Ching Lee's attitude had put there for sometime now.

The older man folded the fans, and took them away, in a safe place, inside a cleaner cupboard, paying not the least any attention to Mickie and his anger.

Only when he realised that the other one had somehow finished he told him to leave as he had work to do. Mickie who was also lingering, hoping that this new assignment might have brought him some extra food, even perhaps some dumplings, no matter if they would have come out from the fridge and the left overs from yesterday's cooking, left the kitchen disappointed, shutting its door with noise.

"Moron", whispered Ching Lee and started the usual work for the day. However, neither his usual energy, nor his everyday zest for it, were around today, and deep lines were all over his forehead, looking somehow harder in the middle of his eyebrows.

He could not take away his mind from the fans. Their stunning beauty, the craftsmanship, and quality of materials, had been sending him back, long time now, where his memory, still unfailing to this subject, was connecting him to his study on the museum days.

Because not for a moment he either believed, or accepted, that these two fans had, or could have, anything to do with Zhung, or his family, even if they were such well off people from those in the old days back home, that could possess really things like those Mickie had brought him. For this he had no doubt, and it was something further than his instinct that had led him to believe this.

Ching Lee spent all morning and afternoon doing all his usual duties like a robot, walking on the same kitchen paths, moving his hands, as he always was accustomed to do, without any noise, or words for anyone, other than

126

what he was forced to exchange with the others at the restaurant as part of the job.

In the evening he left earlier than usually, not lingering to see that everything in the kitchen was left in place, clean and tidy to wait for him for next day's work. However, hardly anyone noticed this, as the young ones were quick to follow him shortly afterwards in leaving the restaurant. The cold was at its worse these days, and apart from very few people working in the area that used to come for a warm lunch, no one else really bothered to come for dinner, as they were in a hurry to return home for some warmth and rest.

Few were also in the underground, and those there were clasping their coats tighter around their bodies for warmth, because even in the train platform, and despite the fact that was many meters under the earth, the chill was coming sharp from the occasional blasts of some wind there, and it was felt like a cutting razor blade deep down to the bones.

Ching Lee felt his face frozen to the point his skin was starting to hurt him.

He grinned his teeth and fold closer his arms to his body. Few people also bothered to read the papers tonight. It was as if everyone in the tube was keeping things close to himself, with perhaps only an apparent interest for some rest and warmth, waiting ahead at home.

Ching Lee looked at the tired faces in the seats opposite his, and some of them looked back at him. It was more or less as if they were all nothing else but theatre dolls that someone has put to sit until their presence was required again.

No matter of his efforts to hang on the other people in the train, Ching Lee's brain had stuck on the two fans in his lap now, making long memory journeys back to those old days again.

From instinct, he knew well that these two fans were not unknown to him. All his efforts were gathered therefore to press his brain more and find where he had seen them, because he knew that he certainly had.

But the years and days had gone, and his memory was slow, like a computer's hard disk that really could not cope with new devices, had all the information stored but it was taking ages to retrieve it.

Suddenly a rip of cold air was blown into his carriage. Heads were swift to lift and look for the source of it, until a young man, quicker than all the others, stormed to the door dividing the carriages, and stretch his arm to close a window open from the other end. He tried a couple of times in vain, as he could not stretch enough towards that direction, until someone from the other carriage saw his effort and got up to help him close it.

"Lunatics" said the young man,"someone obviously must suffer from fever."

"Yes," agreed few voices in the carriage, the others satisfying themselves in watching the scene, if not swearing secretly for the cold wind, which made things worse than they were, only to return afterwards to their usual thoughts when the matter was solved.

Ching Lee got up, preparing himself to get off at the next stop.

Glittering ice was covering outside the small pools of water left from the all day long falling sleet.

He watched carefully his step trying to avoid slipping in one of them." The last thing I need is an accident," advised himself silently."Who on earth I have to look after me, and as for their hospitals, I don't want to be left dying in a corridor."

The thought of what was going to happen to him in a case like this was a constant fear, living inside him always, which though was resulting well in avoiding situations of the kind as hard as he could.

He tightened his coat around his body, as even and in this way the fabric would stretch to provide more warmth, and fastened his step to reach the house as quickly as possible. Outside Abigail's door he stood for some minutes, a low tone quarrelling was coming from inside, and made him to shake his head. Helen's voice was, as

usually, trying to get the upper hand.

He left their door quickly, embarrassed for stopping there, and hurried to get up the stairs.

At the first floor landing the boards gave way under the thin, worn carpet that covered them when he stepped on them. He tripped.

"The bloody man does not want to do anything but collect the rent," Ching Lee cursed the landlord in low voice."We are going to find ourselves downstairs through these boards one day."

It was not a very noisy house tonight, the cold perhaps was giving a hand to this as people were going to bed earlier, and even the voices of Berty and Helen quarrelling mildly, were lost midway up the steps.

Ching Lee hold himself from the balustrade to ascend the next fly of steps, and then he stopped suddenly.

" Canton" he whispered himself,"Canton" he repeated almost immediately,"the Canton museum, that's where I have seen them."

Frozen by his discovery, he lingered in front of the next step, his eyes fixed on the worn texture the green carpet, his brain relieved from a headache that bothered him for sometime. However not all was suddenly gone, as a new fear was coming now to embrace him."How did he get them?" He asked himself, still standing on the same position in front of the steps." He lied, they lied, he has nothing to do with these things. How then did he get them?"

As the questions were pouring into his mind, the one after the other, his pragmatic side realised that it would have been fruitless to stay there, in the first floor landing, trying to find an answer, and slowly began to ascend the stair again, his eyes always fixed, as even this could still provide an answer, to each one of the steps.

The warmth inside his flat was a welcome all too pleasant for his lonely life. Doing all his usual acts of preparation to eat sparingly and go to bed, his mind was still caught on the fans that Mickie had brought today. Now, both of them were lying on his table, which never before had given a basis to such beautiful things.

It must have been well after two o'clock in the morning that finally sleep came to take him.

Before that though, the few moments that in the dark and absolute silence of the place that he used to dedicate thinking of life and people, whatever life and people had been around him, touching then this void of the passing time, now had been nothing else than a more than usual scanning of the past. A meticulous one indeed, where all the images connected to these two fans, as well as some of the previous items he had fixed for Mr Zhung, had to be in a line, and this line had to provide answers to all his questions about them.

Three, or four times he got up again from his bed and went to inspect the fans on the table. The more he was looking at them, the more their image went back into his memory room to match those he had studied at the Canton museum all those years ago. But when certainty about it became the issue, agony replaced quickly the other one of their provenance.

"Was it possible, and how, for someone like Zhung to possess such things? Yes, the man had money, but surely, and for that Ching Lee was damned certain, did not have the taste for a collection of this kind. Was this

his problem? Why he really cared so much? What if indeed Zhung was collecting them?" Wasn't Mickie right to say that all he should care about, was that he would get some extra money? And what if they were stolen?"

He stuck at that a moment that his brain had finally reached what it was looming there, in the background, all this time.

"Stolen? Was Zhung capable for that? He was not clean, somewhere there you could feel it. When though? How?" For the fifth time he got up to look at them.

How could he find out? What could he do, him a poor, old cook? He knew no one to ask for help, so how could he really find out?

The bulk of darkness around him in the room became nothing else but a heavy weight encircling his mind on this state. Why would he care, but then again he wanted to know.

To know.

To know.

He did indeed wanted to know.

Why?

An annoying instinct, like a little devil, wanted to play games with him, and successfully managed to install this inside him.

He wanted to know.

9

Ice, looking like pure snow, was now covering all the pavements, the cars in the streets, the dustbins, the rubbish out of them, boxes, bikes, and everything else that was left outside, changing the usual boring image of this run down neighbourhood into a dreamy, white and glittering one.

Water dripping from every surface that could find available, had frozen and turned into icicles of amazing shapes and beauty, as its drops were hanging under iron bars in fences, or windows, straight up to the rain pipes on walls, gathered on the roofs of the stationary vehicles. As the pale sunshine was making still an effort to warm up a little the world, all those drops that had decided to hang on everything, and everywhere, were now effortlessly transformed into small, shiny diamonds.

A sharp, cold wind, was still overwhelming anything else, making each one of its blows to be felt by the humans and animals around as if a razor blade was cutting their flesh deep down and into the bone.

People were fighting themselves inside their coats, in a useless, most of the time, effort to keep warm.

Ching Lee walked slowly to his usual tube station, his head down so his chin was nearly unseen wrapped inside a thin scarf.

"I really have to use some of the monies I made to buy warmer clothes," he said to himself, thinking also at the same time that this was something that perhaps he should have done before the cold had arrived, as now it was a bit late for that." Nevertheless, I have to do it," he contradicted his previous thought.

He had slept badly last night, tossing every now and then, sweating at times, and at others shivering.

Today he was dragging his feet, and suddenly in his life all those years that he left behind him were now gathered together, counting as a very heavy weight.

The lack of someone close, and even better, someone to trust, to whom he could speak about his findings, was never before more deeply felt.

The years of going on with no other thoughts for anything else, or killing quickly those they dared to come up for that reason, doing nothing else than precisely go on, with whatever this had brought along, were now a sad, long line, where the nothings of family, friends, other people around, were met to haunt him.

What was it all worth for? Wouldn't it not have been better if he had stayed behind with the others?

Were they, his parents, if somewhere, ever, being now pleased that they had saved him, or sad that he was left, as he was, alone, sad, a pathetic little older man, stranger and alien among the millions of people in this country, that he couldn't even called his?

Were they really anywhere to think that, or nothing among nothing was covering now their old lives, as the ashes had done to their big house and other possessions?

"What's wrong with me today?" Ching Lee questioned himself, surprised nearly to be like this, a totally new, run down human, obsessed to the extreme by some findings about a crook.

"Nonsense."

"Was it worth?"

The long line of days, every day in the same rhythm of living, unbroken, strenuous from the repetition of the same, had suddenly become timorous, sad, worn out of agony.

Him, the epitomy of Asian calmness, wisdom, hard work, and silence, endless silence, now was full of nerves, worries, questions that he could not answer.

A sudden noise of a car braking next to him made him jump.

"Hi mate, can we give you a lift somewhere?"

Alarmed, he looked at the direction of the noise and the voice. Berty's head had come out of the half opened window of a small Fiat. Next to him Abigail, all wrapped up in scarf and woollen cap, had fixed her eyes on him.

"Oh, oh, it's you, no, no thank you. I am OK, I am just walking to the tube station."

"You going near Gerrard street, don't you?" Berty continued undisturbed by what the older man had said." I have to collect some things from nearby, why don't you jump in to give you a lift there? It's bloody cold today."

"Yes, yes, it's cold," he repeated like a parrot," you should not bother yourselves with me, I am OK," he replied again timidly, preferring mostly to continue talking with his demons.

"It's not much traffic with this weather, come in, you will be there on time, don't worry about this.

He looked at Abigail, whose big eyes were still fixed on him. She suddenly lift her hand, which was holding a paper butterfly, and she moved it for him inside the glass of the windscreen.

The sight of this child, for whom he had come for the first time on those long years, to care for, made him to look again at both of them, still undecided, a little lost, perhaps uneasy to decide.

Abigail moved the butterfly again, and she smiled to him, with that small, unassuming smile of hers.

" Thank you," he replied quietly,"only if it isn't to put you out of your way."

"No mate, it's OK, I told you that I was going towards your direction. We will only have a small diversion to deliver Abigail to her school."

"But of course."

He sat at the back of the car, and the girl turned her head behind her to watch him. She had no smile now.

" You have not showed me again how to make a butterfly," she reproached him with a low, soft voice." You only did it once but I have not understood it."

Suddenly, all his anxieties had left him for this moment. He was embarrassed by this single, small complain, and looked at her in awe, which he did not have for any other human being.

"Mr Ching Lee is busy with his work," Berty intervened, a little unhappy that his daughter was demanding things from this poor, old chap.

"You are right," Ching Lee told her finally, finding the courage to lift his eyes and looked at her," but I had a lot of problems."

Berty looked at him from the front mirror.

"Are you OK?"

"Oh, nothing wrong with me, other problems," he hesitated for few moments, not knowing what to say.

"Work then?" Asked Berty.

"Work, yes," replied Ching Lee, clinging to the unexpected solution,"yes work."

"Don't pay too much attention to it," Berty's experience in job changing had made him an expert.

"Perhaps," he said to himself slowly, picking up to his previous thoughts"that it would have been much better to take the tube and be left alone". But Abigail had not forgotten her plea, he had no chance.

"Will you show me then?"

"Yes," he said, may be to avoid anything further,"yes, this Sunday coming, in the afternoon, I promise you."

She clapped her hands in joy, and he immediately felt rotten that he had really neglected her, thinking, even for few moments, that he would have preferred to avoid her. When they arrived at Abigail's school, he hurried out to give Berty a hand with the wheel chair.

Berty wrapped his daughter tighter in her coat and started wheeling the chair, when the girl stopped him with a gesture of determination. She then returned to the older man and smiled quietly.

'Will you please push me in?' She asked, clasping again her paper toys in her lap that they were ready by now to roll down.

The two men looked at one another for few seconds.

'Of course' said Ching Lee, and went behind the chair.

It was not difficult to push her. Berty followed them, watching carefully the wheels of the chair on the ice. When they had reached the door, he hurried ahead to open it.

A wave of high temperature, and a strange smell of a not aired place for days, together with an amalgamation of human odours, as well as disinfectant, greeted them. There was noise around and children of all ages, among them some women, determined to put some order, as the day of their charges was starting.

Ching Lee had never been before in all his life in a place like this.

Still holding tight the handles of Abigail's wheel chair, he stopped inside the big, front hall, and feeling numb from what he was seeing.

His head was empty now from anything else.

Any worries from the fans, Mr Zhung, Mickie, Lao Ta, everyone and everything else, had left, leaving room to insert this.

The pose that any disability make you perhaps take in life, either when you see it, or suffer it, was at this moment so grossly enlarged by these small, and other older than Abigail children, some on wheel chairs, others on crutches, some moaning, others crying, some with an indefinite, purposeless laugh hanging like a morose sign of human misfortune from their mouth.

A young boy of around fifteen, was sitting on one of the two chairs in the hall, moving his body on endless movements, backwards and forward, like the vacillating needles of a well wind up pendulum.

Abigail turned around to the older man, 'I am going to this door,' she advised him, and pointed her little finger to a door at the far right end of the hall.

He obeyed, and pushed her chair there with no comment, finding difficult to say anything. Berty followed them.

He was silent too, as for the first time a stranger was allowed to enter this private and sad world of his daughter. More than any other time the sharp pain of guilt grabbed him quietly.

A lady, nurse or teacher, Ching Lee could not distinguish that from her everyday clothes, passed in front of them giving them a half smile of some acknowledgement.

Berty rushed ahead again and opened the door that Abigail had pointed, allowing for the Ching Lee enough room to push the chair in.

Some children were already in the room with a young woman who was entertaining them by showing them big, colourful cards with flowers.

'Good morning Abigail' she said, pleasantly to the girl that did not respond, and leaving the cards on a nearby table, she came to take the girl's chair from Ching Lee to her usual place in the room.

'We will see your father at five then' she told her, giving a curious look to the other man.

Abigail turned towards him, 'I will see you on Sunday for the butterflies?' 'Yes? 'He told her with his usual smile and before she found the opportunity to say anything.

'Yes,' she smiled broadly. Berty bend to kiss her.

When both men were reaching the door, Ching Lee heard Abigail's small voice, 'he is teaching me to make

137

my animals,' she said to the young lady, 'he is so nice.'

He wished he had not to go to work right now, but walk and walk in the frozen city, as even this could have given him an answer to all those things that were happening to him.

He hated to face all those people at the restaurant, do the always same, everyday movements, words, attitudes, situations, actions, his life as he knew it. Everyone and everything. He wanted only to get away, to absorb other things, new people, new situations, actions, gestures, attitudes, words.

Was it the answer?

He stood for a minute there, a soft, sweet pang in his chest, an entirely new feeling, now spreading inside him so beautifully.

'Many thanks mate,' said Berty outside.

'I wish I could do it more often to help you,' he told him.

'Ah, you have already done lots for her. She loves you. She never had since that bloody day any interest for anything.'

'Really?' Ching Lee asked him watching him carefully for the reply, finding that so many things would be depending on that answer.

'My word,' Berty reassured him.

When they sat again in the car, that sweet pang in his heart turned to some very strange feeling of sickness.

'Oh, what after all it would have mattered? To whom all this would be important?'

When they approached Gerrard Street, Berty asked him where he would have liked to drop him. Ching Lee vaguely pointed to the corner before the restaurant, and he thanked him as he got off, the little Fiat wheezed with noise away.

He thought that he really would have preferred to have used the underground. It was good when new things do not come to disturb your inside, when people leave you alone to what you know for so long.

The sickness returned. It was a preliminary pain in the stomach, together with a long desire to throw up, which could not materialize, but was holding him there for time, in that awful condition as it was spreading everywhere.

Lao Ta followed him in the kitchen as soon as he saw him coming. He was in the restaurant from the early hours of this morning to prepare the accounts for the Inland Revenue Inspector that was coming today. He had no time for nonsense, he had to be careful.

'I am going to be in my office for sometime,' he advised Ching Lee, 'I don't want disturbances of any kind. Cook well today, do something special, we have also the Embassy people, they come with some guests. Look after them.'

'Today?' He asked him surprised, 'with such weather?' He thought that perhaps something more was concealed from him, it was odd really for anyone to drop in today of all days.

Lao Ta looked at him angrily, his sliced dark eyes full of annoyance that such an old fool had to express opinions around.

'You see,' he told Ching Lee, his voice hissing, 'they forgot to ask your permission, and decided to come and apologize.'

The older man ignored him.

Lao Ta left the kitchen banging the door behind him. Ching Lee tight his apron straps in his waist, and started the usual duties of everyday, feeling the sickness to penetrate him deeper.

It was hot in the kitchen, as cooker and oven were working in full, and he went to open the door to the backyard. Little he cared for the cold that would have come in, the way he was feeling right now, it would have rather being welcomed. He did not either followed Lao Ta's advice to prepare something special, or bothered for that reason to send someone from the waiters to buy anything from outside. Instead, he did what he would have in his schedule to do, although he did pay extra care in the preparation. Little also he cared about the Inland Revenue Inspector, as in his mind something else was turning, again and again, as he was doing his cooking.

When he reached the restaurant in the morning, Abigail's words, the visit to her school, had given way to the pang inside, clearing the way for one new, small thing.

Someone was waiting for him. Someone needed him for something trivial, but for that also so important. Someone had a feeling for him, out of nothing, and for nearly nothing. His sickness was now no more than this stupid, idiotic things he had to do, which crabbed him for all his days, allowing him not to be able to give some more help to the girl.

All pangs inside for all those kids he had seen today, as well as his little friend, though were quickly giving way to this new kind of something that was rapidly spreading inside him, deriving from them, and filling his entire being with courage and hope.

He wanted to search, he wanted to find out about the fans and the other items, he thought he had some right to this. He should not forget, or push this aside, as he would have done at all other times in such a case, but he should have been persistent and do something about it, to find out as much as he could.

Catching up with his cooking, as he was absorbed in cutting more vegetables for one of his dishes, he dedicated more his talents to a perfect taste of the dish, as if this could have assisted him to achieve his goal.

A joyful, little man, Mr Preston, the Inland Revenue

Inspector, showed up at the restaurant at precisely twelve noon, and headed for Lao Ta's office. He was short, quiet fat, and from the heaviness of his breath one could perhaps detect some kind of heart, or respiratory problem. To the insistence of Lao Ta, who has been transformed in his presence to an angel of kindness and good behaviour, he decided rather pleasantly to join him for lunch at his office, where Mario, the waiter, had already to the instruction of the boss prepared a separate table.

An hour later, six more men entered the restaurant, four men from the Embassy showed up with cigarettes in hand, accompanying two English gentlemen.

Ching Lee spied quietly on them for few minutes behind the small, round window of the kitchen door. He checked on all the three faces, which were familiar to him from the past, and their frequent visits to the kitchen, and then his eyes stopped on the fourth face, which too was a known one, and belonged to an extremely dignified, clever, and well composed young man.

Mr Wang was a counsellor already, despite the fact that he was in his very early thirties, a talented diplomat, for whom any gossip in their society was predicting a very high career in his future.

He was an easy to approach man, however always giving the impression that he was rather becoming aloof and difficult to those that he was sensing they wanted something from him, like Lao Ta, usually looking for favours exploiting his post at the Embassy.

Ching Lee did not know him well, nevertheless in the few times they had met at the restaurant, and the fewer words they had spoken, mostly around food, he had formed the opinion that Mr Wang liked him a little.

Foolish this, or not, he had no other option in finding out, other than approaching him when the right time had come for this.

Mr Wang had been twice on this post of the first counsellor, serving in the interim time back in Beijing as a spokesman for the Foreign office. His career prospects were much brighter now than before, they were not few those expecting him to be the next consul quiet soon. For a man as young as him, ambitions rapidly fulfilled, he was well behaved.

He was nicely dressed too, usually following the eternal classic fashion of all diplomats, in particular the western ones, to whom he had a secret hope to be like one day, he was five feet six inches tall, with a pleasant face. His big, black eyes were kind, but also extremely clever, and penetrating, lit by a sparkle he could not hide should something in the conversation was of particular interest to him. His gold framed glasses were always shown them bigger, and with a depth, that made him when he was looking at you, to feel that whatever was happening you had to tell him always the truth.

Looking at him during his cooking intervals, Ching Lee became more and more reassured that he had to go ahead with his final decision, which was taken from his all day long, painful thinking.

The Inland Revenue Inspector had not left Lao Ta's office, but only once, when he visited the Gents.

'He is smart enough not to take up his words, or accept the accounts he is presenting him for the real ones,' said Mario pointing to him as he saw him going to the toilet, 'he will have a nice meal and nothing. Have you got ready the order for ten?'

'Here it is. Have they finished eating the first course?' Asked Ching Lee, pointing towards Lao Ta's office.

'No, not yet, the inspector is eating well and enjoying it thoroughly,' laughed Mario.

'He is the one to take advantage of him and not the other way. He loved your sweet and sour pork.'

'Good, good, what about the Embassy people? Are they enjoying their meal?"

'I think so. I asked twice and they said that everything was OK. One of their English guests is besotted with your dumplings. I heard him to say two, or three times to the others how good they were.'

'Which of the two?' Ching Lee asked with interest.

'The very tall one with the beard. If I heard well as I was serving them, he is some important man who works with the Government here, or something like that. It seems to me that Mr Wang is in awe of him.'

'How good, how good,' Ching Lee said quietly again.

The restaurant had but three tables occupied, one of which was the one in the centre of his interest. He undo his dirty with stains from various sauces apron, and looked himself at the small mirror that Joy had in the wall of the kitchen to comb his hair ever so often. He passed his hands over his now to keep them straight back, and tidied up his shirt and his sweater.

'I will come to meet them,' he told Mario, who frowned strangely watching him.

'What for?' He asked surprised.

'Lao Ta told me in the morning to look after them.'

'So what, you have done that,' Mario was still surprised by this unusual outing.

'It's different if the chef asks them about the food he prepared, more complimenting.'

Mario burst into laughing.

'So, you are the chef now, oh well then, we should be bowing to you shouldn't we?'

'You are impertinent,' replied Ching Lee, and opening the door went out into the dining area, full of confidence.

Mario followed him with a weird expression to his face, ready to report to Lao Ta any foolishness spoken, or other that the older man might have done.

143

Ching Lee approached the table quietly, but with certainty, a kind smile beaming in his face.

Mr Wang looked at him.

'Was everything all right?' He asked timidly.

'Yes, yes, everything was excellent, we thank you for such nice cooking.'

The big Englishman with the beard gave him a huge laugh.

'Ah, the dumplings were the very best I ever had, I would love to come again even for them only, marvellous, marvellous. What an excellent idea was this Wang to bring us here, great indeed.' He patted him twice on the shoulder with a new warm laugh, and Mr Wang looked at him again with satisfaction decorating all over his young face.

Mario stopped watching and went to serve the other two tables.

'I will be delighted to send you some more, 'Ching Lee told the man who touched his stomach with fear, 'I will explode if I have one more,' he told him, 'I had already far too many.'

'Is there anything else that we can offer you?' He asked them once more, looking only at Mr Wang.

'The bill' he said, and the older man turned around to summon Mario, noticing also that the other three Chinese men on the table kept quiet when he offered more food.

'Perhaps something for you then?' Ching Lee turned again insisting to them.

The shortest of the three men looked at Mr Wang, and still detecting pleasure in his face he said to the cook, 'let's see then what more you have to offer us,' and forced with a greedy, oily laugh Ching Lee to return to the kitchen. Mr Wang frowned, but Zhao had already stand up following the older man on his way back to the kitchen.

'You are very kind,' Mr Wang said when they were

leaving, staying for few moments behind the others. 'Our guests were very pleased, thank you.'

'I am honoured,' he said, and bowed the same way his grand father was bowing to the warlords back at home. He hesitated.

'Mr Wang,' he said timidly, and in a low, whisper like voice, 'you are a very knowledgeable man,' and he looked around as to avoid anyone from hearing him, 'there is a matter that bothers me a lot and I need your advice.'

Mr Wang's eyes became narrow and he looked somewhat annoyed. 'I have no time right now,' he told him rather abruptly, 'as you see our guests are waiting for me outside.'

'But of course,' said obliging Ching Lee, watching at the same time Zhao from the pavement looking anxious at them, 'it's very important though,' his pleading voice had dignity and sounded worried enough.

Mr Wang rushed his hand in one of his jacket pockets, 'here is my card,' he said quickly, give me a call tomorrow, in the afternoon, at about six, I would have finished by that time,' and left to meet the others.

A glorious sunshine bathed London unexpectedly the next day. The chilly air however was still there, penetrating any clothes, and whipping the bodies of those who had to circulate in the streets. But it was so good to find light and some strange, very compensating warmth, whenever a beam of the sun was touching and blessing you.

The last, long, miserable days were soon forgotten, the sunshine being today one of the more frequent topics in the conversations that humans had in this town.

Inside the warmth of the kitchen, Ching Lee little really cared, either for any sunshine, or light, which in any way he could hardly taste where he was. His only encounter with this today was only the short time he had to walk from and to his tube station. All that mattered now was only the kitchen clock, which slowly and intimidating, without fuss, was rolling the time to the afternoon.

By quarter to six, he threw away his apron, put on his coat, and found a quick excuse to disappear out of the restaurant and to the nearest telephone booth. He would have liked to be so much in his flat right now, to speak freely and quietly, and without interruptions, however he had no other option than this.

The telephone rang at the other end for three times, Ching Lee felt his hands sweating in this cold weather, and put the free one to the glass of the cabin to cool it down.

Mr Wang's voice sounded clear and professional like when he finally answered the phone. Ching Lee concentrated now to the cabin's floor, which was full of various rubbish, and in particular on a small, pathetic, and sadly creased chocolate wrapping, whilst he could hear his voice echoing serious and deprived of his body, in an abundance of words that sometimes he was wondering how well his memory had kept. His talk was the one of the scholar and expert he had prepared to be, and looking occasionally from the chocolate wrapping to himself in the glass, he was not certain that this voice still belonged to him.

All this time the silence on the other end had encouraged him, as he thought that perhaps he was not talking to anyone in particular, but to a void, which was making no comments, contradicted, or was angry with him. It was all like talking to himself and it was so good.

He paused when he finished. A long wait, as still no one was speaking to him.

'Mr Wang?' He dared finally, thinking that perhaps they were cut off, and he was indeed speaking to himself.

'I didn't know you were so talented,' the voice said from the other end, 'interesting, very interesting.'

He didn't know what to say, perhaps he was after all very wrong to speak to anyone, perhaps he should have kept everything to him, what a fool he might have been.

'Have you spoken to anyone else?' The voice from the other end asked him.

'No,' he said.

Another silence, which followed, reassured him that he might have been very wrong indeed to speak. To the Embassy? Why on earth he had to involve them? Who else then?

He looked at the people outside, and then looked back at him in the glass.

'I am not so sure what I can really do to help you,' Wang said finally. 'I will think of something though and let you know. Is there anywhere I can contact you other than the restaurant?'

'My home,' said Ching Lee and froze, what if Zhung had good contacts at the Embassy? Ah, what a fool he had been. 'I am hardly there though, I work you see all day, he was quick to add.'

'What time can I find you then? Don't you go back in the evening?'

'Yes,' he had to admit.

'Give me then your telephone number, you do have a telephone don't you?'

'Yes' he said again and gave him the number.

'Listen, I will try to have a search and speak to you as soon as I will have any news, OK?'

Ching Lee did not speak. Now it was his turn to be fearful.

'This is very confidential, please do not reveal my name to anyone,' he said when again found a voice.

'You did well to speak to me,' said Mr Wang, 'I do admire you for this, and thank you.'

He looked outside. More pedestrians were out now, all wrapped up in coats, scarves, hats, gloves, the lot, however there was something hanging to their faces, their walking and movements, a little kind of something extra, like a small extra sparkle flickering around as a reminiscence of this glorious day.

'Thank you,' he told Wang in low voice, 'thank you.'

10

The first signs of spring were showing in the city.

The sun was shining on the buildings below, and old Thames was rolling its dirty, grey and black waters endlessly under the bridges and the big wheel of the London Eye.

Abigail's eyes were full of awe and light. It was a rather permanent illumination this light, spread over her face, body, gestures, the smile she was giving him everytime she was turning towards him to show him one more spot in the horizon, one more building that she was considering having a funny shape, or that it was more attractive to her.

'It was mainly a green town,' thought Ching Lee, 'with the exception of some domes, like the one of the Imperial War museum, or that one of St. Paul's.

The light brown bulk of the Houses of Parliament with the clock of Big Ben, the quays with the trees, all green and pretty, Cleopatra's column, yes those, the last ones were giving London a pretty sight, but only those on that side. The rest,' he thought with disappointment, 'is full of big, ugly buildings, no more, no less.'

The sun was flickering on metals, the glass of the buildings, the waters of the river.

Ching Lee stood there, inside the cubicle, holding himself from the bar, and hanging his glance everywhere beneath him. Abigail and Helen did not exist a lot right now. He was pleased to bring his little friend here, pleased that he had thought of it as an item of entertainment for a confined in a chair sad, little life, something to give her pleasure which certainly the others living with her never thought of. But once this was achieved, and he saw that on the girl's face, the time had returned to him.

He could not understand if it was the impact of this huge town beneath his feet, or the fact that he, Ching Lee, an older Chinese immigrant with such a distant past that had only survived as a frightening memory, the no present, other than the dullness of the restaurant, and certainly little apart from nothing future, had finally made something. He has been connected with another human being. He had feelings, interest, and a day to think about every morning.

'This city will never be mine,' told himself, as now the white body of St. Paul's, the OXO Tower, the egg shaped London Authority, and the city around them, was slowly sliding, as the wheel was turning, bringing their cubicle closer to the ground.

'Yet, I have it in me. What is it doing there? This thing inside? This was not Nanking, will never be. These people around were not his people. They looked different, spoke another language, had another religion, lived in different houses, and ate other kind of food. I know them though. I see these buildings often, I like the river, it's fun their language which I speak everyday, I live in one of their houses.'

'Look, look Mr Ching Lee, look at the clock, we move away now, don't we?'

He turned and smiled to her, 'yes' he answered, 'we do.' Did you like it?'

'Oh yes,' Abigail's voice was reflecting all the excitement she had. Helen was keeping silent, something which the older man found both a blessing and a break

from the usual chatterbox attitude.

She had also been overwhelmed by the view of the big city from up there. In her restricted too life and enjoyment of it, this was the exception she so warmly welcomed.

It was a bright colour in the horizon beyond the Houses of Parliament when they got out of the wheel. 'Dusk too

150

had its beauty,' Ching Lee thought pushing Abigail's chair along the river banks, and then looked for a passage to get on the Westminster Bridge to call a cab. Frustrated by the steps, he noted to Helen to follow the other direction towards the back of the old GLC building.

Abigail's improvement of attitude, disposition and will towards her small life, were giving doctors a higher hope. 'Not that it would have ever being possible for her to abandon her chair, but being mentally and psychologically feeling better' they informed her parents.

Her transfer, with a lot of difficulty and pressure from Berty's side, to a better and more understanding school, with children with a lot lesser problems than those in the old one, had given her a lift of spirits which Ching Lee thought that were but a miracle for his little friend. Many times he was looking at his paper toys, which now had expanded from his part in design, combination of colours and quality, in awe, about the power that could inflict on such a small soul.

'God, gods are here,' his mother used to say, always looking with doubt at the various stone ones in the temple, lowering her voice.' We just do a duty to them,' and she was secretly pointing to the stone ones, this is how we found things, better not to disturb them, but they are only here, everyday, and the demons too.'

Berty had been good too, it was as even the first sights of his daughters improvement had provided him with courage to overcome guilt and his motionless attitude towards any help. Something like a shame, which Helen hardly ever showed towards Ching Lee, and his efforts to amuse Abigail had also provided an even stronger incentive to do something for her.

The Lotus flowers were spread evenly on the silk leaf.

He cast his eyes on them and forgot anything else around for a long time.

It was a garden, it was painted like a garden, all around them, so elegant, so beautiful, so faded from time, that it was making him to look at it as if it was a dream, all wrapped up in a cloud, in the mist of forgotten happiness. There was nothing here to bother him at such moment, nothing and no one else existed, and a smile, broad, happy, beaming with something like a sublime, out of this world, sense was now covering his face.

There were so beautiful these fans that could really take your breath away.

No, he was determined, absolutely determined that he had to uncover the whole truth behind anything which could have been the reason for someone to mistreat such wonderful things.

Last Sunday he spent all afternoon with Abigail again. It had become a habit now, and the Morton's were treating him like an old friend. It was good.

Him and Abigail, had both occupied a corner of the Morton's sitting room, with Helen, Berty and the boys, occupying themselves between the kitchen and their rooms, providing the girl and her newly found teacher, with peace for concentration.

She was not a very fast learner, but he was amazed with her dedication to learn.

Their small conversation, which had come as a sheer surprise for her family, was the only one he had come to enjoy in these days of life. The small words, the innocent phrases, the numerous questions on things and their existence around, were like her small toys always hanging from her lap, hands, chair.

Abigail smiled ho him so many times today as more and more the tiny animals and fans, that were her latest joy, had started to take shape in her hands.

It was for her.

It was for his little friend that that long feeling, spreading everywhere inside him, flat, grey, and monotonous, his constant existence of nothing, had started slowly to take lightly shades of colour.

So, it was also the courage built in low space, to do something, to be of use, to achieve, even only this, a search for his fans, a reason for their provenance, an excuse for fighting.

Was that so important?

'Can my animals walk someday?' Abigail had asked him. He had looked at her, not knowing what to say, as his hands were helping hers in shaping slowly the colourful paper.

'Will they?' She hold his hand, stopping him from doing any further movement until he could have given her a reply. 'Will they?'

His delicate objects have never taught him to reply on such questions. His education was deficient, his knowledge on the kitchen counter helpless and poor.

'Will they?'

'Perhaps,' he had dared, 'if they want to do it someday, I think it's possible.'

She had smiled, and like a butterfly in the light, her wings had entered without noise his heart.

Mr Wang had been waiting for news back from home.

His hunting dog nose had smelled that this was an interesting case. He believed the honesty of the older man, for whom his information was more than impeccable.

'A quiet old thing, he cooks very well, his recipes are back from the old capital, sort of out of date but extremely tasty, and he likes to make fans, or repair them mostly really.'

The information was complete really.

Wang had good friends in some Ministries back home, it would have not taken time to find out a little more.

He looked relaxed and content. Rumours had it that a new promotion would have not been that far away. He could wait, there were no anxieties about it, as long as everything was in line, and so far it has been proven that this was the case.

If now something good for those bureaucrats back home had come up as extra, so much the better.

He looked outside the window of his office.

For a boy of poor background, he had not done badly. His father's determination to see him change his life, change the old path of worries, problems, poverty, had worked well.

Wang thought of his father with a feeling of gratitude. He had managed to change life for all of them. He had come from his village in the north, an impoverished young man in his twenties, to the new capital Beijing. His work as servant, carrier of groceries, cleaner, butcher, and finally very low level clerk of the government, had brighten his horizon, had helped him to meet other people, some of them providing him with some assistance to enlarge his means, and connections, and to raise his three children in a more comfortable way that allowed them to go to school.

But from the other two, it was him, Wang, who had inherited his will, stubbornness, wit, and endeavour, to go even higher than him in life.

His sister, was a pretty girl who had not a lot in her brain, she married very young, found a small job at the local government, and before even being twenty- two, had also two children, and thought that already her life had fulfilled its role.

So did his brother, and both of them, as much as they satisfied the family that certainly would be better off in life than Mr Luo, their father, still had not given him the big flying feeling that did him, Wang. He was the one who wanted to study, so his father had done his best to help, and when he had entered, to the delight or everyone in the family, the Foreign Office, Mr Luo's happiness was more than complete.

The trees in Portland Place had already lots of new leaves. Spring was not only beckoning, but had come slowly to stay.

Topping his fingers on his desktop, Wang thought of his past of thirty- three years, like a small, black and white documentary, which someone was rolling its tape quickly, on the polished wood of his desk, and the few branches of the trees he could see outside his window.

The telephone's crisp, loud ringing startled him. He switched off the tape playing inside his head, and quickly cleared his mind for the next job.

A member of staff in the Cultural Department of the Embassy advised him that they had just received an e-mail from the Ministry at home, which he thought, might have been of interest to him.

Wang returned to the screen of his PC, always on the side of his desk, and he started to scroll the mouse.

'Indeed, it had been noticed for sometime that several art crafts have been missing from several museums in the country, the police was investigating now for sometime. It was very interesting the information they had received from the Embassy. Mr Cao Yasha, their advisor on this type of art objects, would be soon going to Unesco in Paris. Would it have been possible to view some of these items, during his stop over in London?'

Wang read again the message, to be certain he had not misunderstood anything. 'Sometimes,' he thought, 'luck is also coming around to help, not bad not bad at all.'

He lift the telephone, and press one of the internal connection buttons.

'Yes, I saw it,' he said to someone on the other end, 'I will take it up from here, and reply to them as I know the people involved, leave this to me.'

He hang up, and tapped again his fingers on his desktop, as he always used to do when he wanted to compose himself for serious thought and decision. He tapped a little longer, and he plunged his eyes deeper on the polished wood, and as if this was the only advise the wood could reflect back, he looked at his watch for few seconds.

'He would be still at the restaurant, 'informed himself, in a voice that only him and his desk could hear, 'no it's not wise, only tonight.' He turned to the screen of his PC, and clicked on the small window, 'reply.'

'They would welcomed of course Mr Yasha, it was a tremendous opportunity to assist this way their investigation, however they had to contact again the individual who had seen these items, and advise back as soon as possible.'

'Tonight, 'he said, loudly this time, and searched his notepad for a number he had written there some days ago.

The doctor stroke lightly Abigail's hand, which had been resting for sometime into hers.

She was a short, plump woman with yellow hair, which had no connection with anything blond, but mostly with those children's crayons, with thick, strong colours, leaving behind wide strokes on paper.

'You do like your new school, don't you?' She asked the girl, however this not as part of her dutiful questions, but rather from genuine interest.

'Yes,' she replied, 'it has lots of light, and I do have also my own desk, I can make more of my animals there.'

'Good,' said the woman, 'that's why we wanted you to go there.'

'Are you certain doctor that this is not going to cause her more anxieties now?' Helen still, did not like to accept that Abigail had entered a new phase in her small life.

'Abigail Mrs Morton,' said Dr Bessan in a cool, low voice, 'is improving fast,' she left the girl, and walked around her, changing her voice into a whisper that only her, and the girl's parents could hear, 'of course we know she will not walk again, but now she has an interest for things, she is pleased she can do something with her hands, she speaks and expresses herself. Isn't that important? What more we could have expected, she is getting slowly out from her trauma, at least she can understand that she is like any other normal girl of her age. Eventually she has to come to terms with her disability by accepting that this is the bitter reality, but where she is now she will meet other kids with whom she can talk something more substantial other than little cries, or screaming.

Your daughter has a healthy mind, however what happened to her has registered deeply and effect her inside, this is extremely traumatic for a kid that until then used to play and run.

Isn't it better that now can identify herself with many other kids, and she is capable of learning again?'

'Yes, yes, but of course,' said Helen a little embarrassed, but still in full doubt that her daughter was closer now, at least in her head, to a more normal kid.

'You cannot easily find people to have the will to help children, this guy, your husband told me about, must really love Abigail, to help her so much.'

'Well, he taught her how to make these small, paper animals, that was all,' said Helen, dismissive in attributing to Ching Lee a better role, and irritated that Berty had already spoken to the doctor of a stranger who had managed perhaps to achieve more than either of them ever had.

'No,' said Berty crossed, as even he had understood what was looming inside her, and who so far had not said a word, 'you have to be fair. It might be nothing to you but the guy gave her interest, personal interest, it was for her only any attention, and it was not a small thing to teach her something. She was hardly speaking to any of us before, now she does, she tells us what she feels, she plays with her brothers. We could not have done what he did. If you think that this is small, you are wrong, it is important to her, very important.'

Helen tighten her lips, a sign that she was angry with her husband, how dare he to retort her like that? What about all the things she had done?

'I tend to agree with your husband,' said the doctor smiling but not pleased with her, and walking behind Abigail's chair, she stroked her hair.

The telephone was ringing in the silence of the flat as soon as Ching Lee put his key in the lock of his door. Surprised and shocked as even he had discovered that a ghost was inside, he hesitated what to do, then he calmed down, it surely was not his, might have been somewhere else, possibly one of his neighbours, he found difficult to connect himself that it was his own phone ringing, but as he opened the door, the ringing clearly registered now that was coming out of his front room. Still hesitant he went quickly and picked it up.

'Is this Mr Ching Lee?' A man's voice asked kindly.

'Yes' he replied, 'who are you?'

'Wang here,' replied the voice, 'your telephone was ringing for sometime, I thought that you would have been still at the restaurant.'

'I just came back, this minute.'

'I am sorry for disturbing you but certainly I thought it was better to speak to you at the privacy of your home.'

'It's all right sir, no problem, you did not disturb me at all.'

'Look,' said Wang, who thought that he already had done enough on preliminary politeness, 'I spoke to some officials back home, there are some important artefacts missing from museums in the country, you might be right you know, but as you understand this is only an assumption, we cannot run into conclusions of any kind, as the whole matter requires a lot of investigation.'

'But of course,' Ching Lee stuck his eyes on the unfolded fans on his dining table, with that thin, membrane like paper covering them to protect them from any dust as he was on the process of repairing them, 'I was right, I was right' said to himself.

'First of all this matter should stay between ourselves, it's a very important issue, delicate, as well as highly confidential, we do deal with our country's government here, we have to be careful.'

'I realise this, this is why I only talked to you.'

'Good, I appreciate it. Look, an expert of the Ministry of Culture is coming around in two weeks time, I was asked if possibly could show him these items, so I am afraid you have to bring them around to the Embassy when he comes, I 'll let you know exactly the time. Could you do this? I am afraid you have to.'

'Two more weeks?' Ching Lee asked, aiming this question mostly to him than Wang.' They are nearly ready, how can I keep them any longer? His assistant already asked today for them.'

'That's up to you only. I cannot help in this. Can you do it?'

Ching Lee looked again towards the fans on the table, things had started taking a different road now, one that he could not control. It might have been harmless for him, it might be not though be like that for long. Now, this guy who had followed his fears all the way, had transformed them into something new, very real and difficult to change. Why on earth had thought to speak to an Embassy man, all this trouble, how would it finished, where things could lead from here onwards?

'Are you there?' Wang asked a little crossed that no reply had been given to him.

'Yes,' he said finally reluctantly, 'I heard you Mr Wang.'

'So?'

'I will try sir, but..'

'What?'

'This has to be very confidential.'

'I was the one who said it first, wasn't I?'

'Yes.'

'I understand your fears,' Wang paused, 'if the whole thing is as you have suspected, we have to be more careful, you in particular. I am not the police here, I can only speak for myself, but I will try to help you, as much as I can that is.'

'Thank you.'

'I can tell them therefore that their expert can see them.'

'I'll do my best.'

'That's good. I'll let you know when you should bring them to my office.'

'Yes.'

'Good night now then.'

'Good night sir.'

He placed carefully the receiver from his hands on the appliance, his palms were a little wet, 'it's getting rather warm,' he thought, and then he proceed to carry on with his usual functions of every evening. Things were only trying now to untangle inside, he had time, a little more time. But for what? It was hardly possible for him now to stop.

After he finished his dinner, he sat on the table and worked for a while in one of the fans. Dealing with those gorgeously pierced sticks, the mother of pearl on them still intact from the passing of time, the small precious stones glimmering on the light, the little faces, all with different expressions on the figures there, all the figures different really, a scene, a real life scene from a time gone and lost forever He gasped for his breath.

Why on earth he had to do that?

But he had to do that.

Everyone should respect this work. It should be high on people's admiration, these were the most beautiful, most precious, admirable, pieces of art, and no one should treat them as Zhung.

Sleep was not coming fast. His feet were tired, he had noticed they got a little swollen now and then.

In the darkness of his bedroom distant noises from the road were disturbing the stillness of the space.

Ching Lee laid in his narrow bed, eyes wide open in the dark. Some dim suspicion of a light, coming occasionally from the cars outside and through his rather not thick curtains, was slightly illuminating the ceiling, and the dusty paper shade of the light.

Now it was done, and there was no way really to go back. Why he had to stir up such turmoil?

If Zhung was indeed guilty, what then? Accused and arrested wouldn't he have his people to go after him? Wasn't everything all right so far, why, who he really thought that he was to disturb things around?

Sleep was not coming.

Despite the voices inside him being supportive and approving, there was another one of them, looming in the background, condemning and accusing him for having no right to upset things but should have left them as they were.

And what if it was for that reason indeed that he wanted to do it? The same thing, which was buried all those years inside, was now fighting to come out, and show everyone that this no one human being was someone sometime, like those that were now important, a person with a good family, wealth, knowledge. The small, unknown cook of

161

London's Chinatown, him, the isolated old man of a tiny one bedroom flat in Camden, had guts and courage to fight and expose a powerful crook.

And what if Zhung's contacts were expanding to the Embassy's staff, and the whole story was already drawn into swallow water, before even being able to see any light?

He closed his eyes, and pressed keeping down his eyelids, perhaps sleep now might have been more benevolent and come again tonight. But the continuous tick-tack of his bedside clock, was a noisy witness as it was counting his time, that sleep had forgotten him, at least for now.

Past three in the morning, he gave up, got up and went to the table at the sitting room, switching on the lamp on top of the fans.

There they were again, his babies, his children, his lovers, his family. And here they were with their colours, their precious stones, their elaborate carving, their little figures playing life, all in their sublime beauty.

Where these exquisite items could have end up if it was not for him to care for them? A collector's cabinet display, a woman's hands, an antique dealer's window, or on the coffee table of a rich American couple?

They had only one chance to go back where they belonged, to be with all the other things in that vast, other times happy for him, country, which so many times now he was even forgetting that it was his own.

He took away the slim cover, and with a gesture as light as the touch of a bird's feather, stroked their sticks and leaf with his forefinger.

No lover ever stroked the skin of his loved one with such adoration, a happy, endless smile hanging from the light opening of his lips.

He was the one, the one and only to protect them.

Regrets now?

No.

None.

There was nothing else that he could have really done.

'An honest man is always an honest man, poor or rich,' his father used to say, 'and even if they bury you inside a treasure, you should always do the work written in the consciousness of the honest man. There is nothing more important in life than being able to sleep when you go to bed in the evening.'

He stopped smiling.' Why then this was not possible now?'

'Fear,' told him the voice looming still in the background, 'fear which occupies, and kills the soul.'

He stretched all the muscles in his body, which they lifted him from bending over the fans, gathered any courage he had left, and switched off the light.

'There was nothing more that I could have done,' he said, and his voice fall in the room with some extraordinary power, 'nothing else, and I had enough for now, time to have some sleep,' and tripping occasionally on the furniture, found again his bed in the dark, and got quickly under the duvet, which luckily has kept there the warmth of his body from before.

'Let him reap what he has sown, time comes for everyone when they answer for their actions.' And as if this, within the darkness of the room, and after having touched his beloved items, whose feeling of beauty still he carried under the skin of his forefinger, the dim lights of the passing outside cars, were all working like the sweet notes of a lullaby, long forgotten in memory, sleep came finally, benevolent and continuous to claim him for the rest of the night.

11

'I have an appointment with Mr Wang,' Ching Lee told timidly one of the receptionists at the Embassy.

The man looked at him strangely, whilst two others sitting at the back behind the counter, were carefully watching him.

'Do you have an appointment? With whom you said?'

'Mr Wang,' he repeated.

'Wang who?' Asked the man again, starting to get a little angry.

He searched frightened his raincoat pocket taking out a small card, 'Mr Wang Sang,' he said, more certain of the name now.

The man at the front of the desk looked again at his old raincoat, and then to his face, however he picked up the phone, looking at the same time at a big book open on top of the counter. Ching Lee could not see the phone hidden as it was beneath the counter-desk.

'I have Mr Ching Lee here,' said to someone at the other end, 'he says he is seeing Mr Sang at nine thirty,' still doubtful about the appointment of this shabby old man, from what he could considered, and despite the fact that he had already discovered the name and the appointment in his book.

Ching Lee looked around at the vast hall.

He was not feeling well since last night, and he had slept badly, as even some kind of knot formed by hundreds of nerves, which were gathered by in his stomach, and stayed there without any intention of moving.

'I will send him up,' said the man with the phone at whoever was in the other end, without taking off his eyes from him all the time that he was speaking.

Ching Lee dared to look at him too.

'You go up the steps,' he told him, 'second floor, they will meet you there.'

The others grinned at the back.

'Thank you,' he said.

Then, the other one behind the counter saw the bag.

'You have to leave this here,' he told him.

He froze.

'I am sorry,' his voice trembled, 'but the instructions I had, were to take this back to him.

'We have to look inside.'

Ching Lee hesitated, and then approached the counter and opened the bag.

The man looked at him more strangely than before now, the others stopped grinning, he tried to put his hand inside, Ching Lee was quick now.

'These are very delicate items, you may look but not touch them, if in doubt, please call Mr Sang now,'however on this no one dared to contradict instructions from upstairs, and they finally let him go.

He went to the steps, and he started slowly ascending them, holding tightly the handle of the balustrade with his free hand, and thinking that if he had delayed perhaps for few more moments there, things might have turned to something perhaps unpleasant for him. Fear was all over inside. The staircase was like climbing a tall mountain, going up in effort its dangerous surface, an effort that was really very painful as he was struggling not to fall.

All the three from the reception were watching closely his back. He certainly was a type to enter their attention here, such different visitor from the others in dressing and manner, it was but an interesting curiosity element in their dull work behind the counter. Occasionally, the power to examine visitors, had been registered as some extraordinary capacity they thought they had, which had led them to believe that perhaps they too should have been advised in detail for any work taking place upstairs. Ching Lee could feel their eyes penetrating his back, all three pairs of them, and felt that perhaps this was going to continue for sometime, little as they had to deal with him, their curiosity being perhaps increased by this reason, so the best he could do for now it was to forget them all together.

But fear, which had come to overtake him, and the more it was spreading inside, the more everything in this big building was contributing in enlarging it, the receptionists, the staircase, the silence around, above all the bag in his right hand.

If he was ever asked about the time duration of ascending those steps from the ground to the first floor, he could hardly say. He believed that it was a very long portion of time indeed, its braking into something more realistic was impossible.

When he finally reached the top, a young and smiling girl, came to meet him. She was kind and eager to help. Her smile, which had nothing to do with the grinning of her colleagues downstairs, melted for seconds the fears inside.

'They are waiting for you,' she informed him, and after her little chat about the steps and the weather, she proceeded to open doors for him.

He stopped just before she opened the door of Wang's office.

'Mr Sang is expecting you, 'she smiled to him again.

'We all know him at the restaurant as Mr Wang, 'he stammered stupidly.

'That's his small name,' told him the girl.

'Oh yes,' he said.

'That's all right,' she replied for no reason, and opened the door of a room, where he could see the back of two men sitting in a table with some empty chairs around.

'Mr Ching Lee,' she announced him to the men, and made room at the door for him to get in.

Both men turned quickly towards the sound of her voice. Ching Lee hold himself from the door's frame, as if the wood there could, by sustaining him for few seconds, to provide him also with courage.

Wang got up and approached him, his hand already stretched for a handshake.

Clumsily the bag changed hands in order to free his right hand.

'Thank you for coming,' Wang said smiling, and noted to the girl to bring some tea, who left trying to close the door behind her, however he stood there, not knowing what to do, as he was standing still half way out of the door, his other half inside.

'Please, please come in, 'Wang nearly pushed him in so the girl can close the door.

The other man was watching carefully.

He was an old man with white, thick hair, which harsh as they were, standing up on his head, were forming some kind of halo, or may be, regarding from the angle you were looking at him, an upright brush sitting there on top of this man's head without any purpose.

His thin glasses were framed elegantly by gold frame, and his eyes behind them big and dark brown, kindly rested on Ching Lee's figure for sometime.

'This is Mr Cao Yasha,' Wang pointed to the man, who smiling tend his hand to Ching Lee too.

'Welcome Mr Ching Lee, we thank you very much for taking the time to come.'

He shook his hand, and both with Wang pulled out a chair next to the one Mr Yasha was sitting, and showed it to him, he obeyed, and sat down, still the bag in his hand as if it was briefcase carrying a million pounds in it..

'We thank you for what you are doing, you should not

be afraid for anything, on the contrary be very proud for what you do.'

His accent and voice were soft, for Ching Lee they were both a sound from the past, the way the educated people used to speak at that long, lost time.

A wave of politeness and genuine kindness was oozing from his body, voice and face, and slowly made Ching Lee to forget his fear attack, anxiety, and agonies, and return slowly to the man he used to be, reflecting on the same line of waves with this man, speaking on the same kind of way he knew so well, extending what was used to be a kind of life in a bygone era to this office in central London.

Wang was carefully watching both, a little startled from this immediate rapport between the two men, and reconfirming to himself that Ching Lee was someone different from the old cook at the 'Dragon's Head' in London's Chinatown. A slight bewilderment was now in place as to who really Ching Lee was.

'I see' said Mr Yasha, 'that you are a very well educated man, how does did it happen to leave our country?'

'This is a very long story,' he replied, 'I don't think I will very much like to remember it,' he stopped and looked at the very well polished wood of the table, 'I don't mean to be rude, or anything else, difficult perhaps, 'he stopped again as if to catch his breath, 'but it is a painful story for me.'

'I am sorry,' said Cao Yasha, 'I didn't mean to be intruding to your life, but as you may understand, you come out as someone who little has to do with his present occupation, so one is made to wonder, and you know, we humans are always curious for others.' He laughed a little, still in a rather warm manner.

'I come from a good family, my father and grandfather were well educated too, but life change's, that's all, not all of us have luck.'

'Yes, yes, how true, 'said Mr Yasha, and his eyes forgot for few seconds Ching Lee, and plunged into what it seemed some kind of unpleasant thought.'

'Here are the fans,' Ching Lee put abruptly the bag on the table, and opened it slowly with his usual religious carefulness. He spread the thin, muslin like cover he used on them when he was not working, and spread it on the table, then the fans were opened the one after the other.

'Oh,' said Mr Yasha, and bent carefully over them examining the leaves, the sticks, and pivot.

Ching Lee approved that he did not touch anything, and frowned when after a while the other changed his mind, and still carefully, picked them up to examine them closer. Neither Wang, nor Ching Lee said anything.

When he finished, he placed them again where they were before on the table, and produced from a large briefcase a brown envelope. He took out some photographs, which he spread on the table.

'Do you recognise any of these items?' He asked Ching Lee.

Ching Lee took them in his hands and looked carefully. Two mirrors, three boxes with good stones on the lid, some more fans. He sat back at his seat, a white colour spreading with speed all over his face.

'I have fixed this, and this, and this, and this,' he said quietly, and pointed to all the items he knew so well.

'And here are these fans too, 'said Mr Yasha, and produced out of his briefcase one more envelope with more photographs.

Ching Lee took from him the three photos showing the fans from behind a glass, museum case.

He stretched his body in the chair, 'I knew it,' he told them calmly, 'that's why I spoke to Mr Wang, I am sorry

Mr Sang, he corrected. 'There were times that I thought perhaps my old mind was playing funny stories at me, however on many other times I was so certain.

'They were stolen from several museums of China, in Beijing, Nanjing, Guangzhou, Suzhou, Guangxi,' Mr Yasha said, and from various others, less known museums. It's been sometime that we have tried to get any information, or really anything about these items, and I am sorry to say, it appears that people from inside the museum have helped. However we have no concrete proof. 'He turned to Ching Lee, his face now serious and determined.

'Who is this person Mr Ching Lee?' He asked now in his official voice.

'He is called Zhung, we call him Mr Zhung at the restaurant, he is a business man, and has an assistant, Mickie. He brings me the items to fix. He is rich, at least everyone at the restaurant says so, our boss Mr Lao Ta is very impressed by him.'

'Did he ever say what are these items to him, that he brings you to fix?'

'Yes, mostly items that belonged to his late mother, and his family, and that he wants them fixed for his ancestors sake. I believe he has left to be understood that he comes from an old, wealthy family.

Mr Yasha exchanged a look with Wang, got up and went to the window, looking for few minutes outside.'

'You have a lot of courage,' he said, I reckon this is a very nasty story that we have to investigate a lot. Are you willing to help us?'

'Sir, 'Ching Lee said quietly, 'I thought I have already showed you that.'

'I am sorry, I didn't mean really any offend.'

'I understand.'

Mr Yasha turned from the window to Wang, 'you have to

help him and us here,' he told him, 'and protect this man as much as you can.'

'I will do my best, however you understand I cannot act like Scotland Yard.'

'Do your best,' Mr Yasha repeated in a way of an order, which sounded as an imminent threat for things to happen ahead.

Mr Wang looked irritated, but also shut into what was part of his scheme, and which now could not escape.

Mr Yasha returned again to the fans on the table. He bent over them, then slightly raised them again, and he looked at them carefully from all angles.

Wang and Ching Lee were watching his movements, their eyes like those of two dolls, who scroll their glass up, down, right, left. The sun from outside was bathing the room with light.

Ching Lee thought that time in some way was not moving, it was not doing anything, and if somehow it could be measured, it would have been nothing more than a straight line, like those that a cardiogram is producing when the heart does not work anymore. A long straight line, without ups and downs, minutes, seconds. Since he came, the same question was constantly repeated in his brain, 'why? What am I doing here?'

Finally Wang, always conscious about the passing of every minute, realised that he had lots of others things to deal with for the day, this matter being only something small to be used in future to his advantage, decided to end the ceremony of examinations by discreetly looking at his watch, only to say concerned, 'we do not want Mr Ching Lee dismissed from his boss, do we?' And he laughed with a small, rather embarrassed laugh, 'I am afraid it's ten thirty already, and he has to return back to work. I am terribly sorry,' and turned to a more serious tone, 'Mr Yasha to bring this up, but if something happens it will make things worse, we want things only to show as they were.'

Ching Lee could have not been more pleased, 'I have to be at the restaurant as quickly as possible,' he backed Wang's comment.

Yasha lift his head and looked at them both, 'one needs a little more time to establish for certain such a serious matter,' he told them scornfully.

Wang sat back at his chair frowning and regretting what he had said, 'after all this was for him too, to hell with Ching Lee's job and his others affairs for the day. Ching Lee's agony returned now to time limits as he knew them, and Lao Ta's thought, who would have not be happy at all if everything in the kitchen was not prepared on time. All of a sudden time had come back as an incongruous element in the room.

'You have done a brilliant job,' Yasha decided finally to leave the fans on the table.

'Thank you,' Ching Lee said.

'You like fans so much?'

'Yes sir.'

'You always did?'

'Yes.'

'You are an astonishing good fan repairer.'

'That's very kind of you to say so.'

'Have you studied this?'

'Yes.'

'What really have you studied?'

'History, and history of art, Chinese of course I mean for both, and I took a special study to repair some works of art too, fans in particular,' he stumbled now.

'Did you come to this country in the mid sixties didn't you?'

Ching Lee stopped for few seconds to breath, no one else had ever asked all these years so directly anything like this, there was no way now to allow it.

'Has this got to do anything with this?' He asked in a very straightforward manner, and pointed to the fans.

'No, no it doesn't, 'Yasha replied and bent his head to look now over the fans.

'Yes, I did,' suddenly Ching Lee's voice filled the room with boldness, 'yes I did, as the gangs beat my father to death, and set up our house on fire. I did, as they were all gone to save me. What more do you want to know now?' The high tone of his voice vibrated the walls of Wang's office with anger. 'Are you perhaps one of them? What more do you want from me? I brought you what you wanted, but not because of you, or anyone else, not even for what you now call our country, our home, I did it for them, and he stepped towards his fans. 'They were the only things that kept me alive, I don't want to see them mistreated in the hands of crooks, cheap tradesmen and others, I don't care who. They should be where they belong as they carry on them hundreds of years of civilisation, that's all.'

He sat back at his chair, out of breath and astonished for this man he had always thought gone for good, but he was still carrying inside.

Wang was a little pale.

Mr Yasha removed his glasses, took a handkerchief out of his pocket, and started cleaning them. When he was satisfied that the level of cleanness he wanted was achieved, he put them on again and returned the handkerchief back to his pocket.

He went to the window and looked outside.

'Spring must be beautiful here as well,' he said, however no one gave him a reply.

'My mother was a teacher Mr Ching Lee,' he said quietly, 'so was my father. She was beaten by those gangs, I presume the same ones you were referring. She gave birth immediately afterwards to a dead baby, and then she died too. My father was humiliated publicly and he committed suicide. I was alone.'

He stopped.

For once more in the day, time had left everything and everyone in the room.

Ching Lee stuck his eyes on the guard sticks of the closed now fans, Wang was unhappily watching the chairs and the other furniture around, he had not plan for reminiscences of any kind, these in particular.

A void was scattered everywhere.

'We are two of the same kind,' Mr Yasha decided to speak again, 'we only had different luck, that's all.'

'Ching Lee looked at him, 'I am glad now you understand perhaps,' he told him quietly, the anger in his voice giving way to his usual quiet manner again.

'I do,' said the other.

'Sir' said Wang, but Yasha stopped him with a movement of his hand, 'I know what I wanted to know,' he said, 'you may take back the fans Me Ching Lee, I suppose with the official procedure not yet in place, we are not in a position to make a claim on these fans. If you could delay their return for a little while, we would be immensely grateful, however we cannot force anything before the Ministry advises officially the authorities here.'

'So, we are certain,' said Wang, pleased that things finally reached a conclusion, and much to his benefit.

'Yes,' Yasha replied, turning back to face them both. 'Mr Ching Lee was absolutely right that these are stolen museums items, and I have every proof I need for my report, which I will prepare today.'

He went back to his briefcase, opened it and brought out a small camera, then, he went back to the fans on the table and photographed them. He left the camera on the table, and placed his hand on Ching Lee's shoulder.

No one said anything.

Wang stretched his chest muscles, and watched for few minutes these two old men standing there with their remote and unexpressed faces. No one was facing the other, Yasha's hand being forgotten on the other's shoulder.

12

The plane trees were full of leaves, their shade covering big areas on the small square.

Their tall, green presence was providing the surrounding area with the tone of countryside airs, welcomed by most, usually others than the streets cleaners who had to collect their masses of fallen leaves in the autumn.

The crocuses had come and gone, some late ones were only hanging still here and there, reminiscences of the yellow, mauve, and white carpet that was decorating the square weeks ago.

Daffodils were out for sometime now, their slim, tall bodies, tantalising with the slightest blow of the wind, like regular pendulums.

Martha Nickolls sat for few minutes, coffee mug in hand, behind the window, watching carefully on the small square the movements of the passers-by, the leaves on the trees, the flowers on the ground.

During her little, free occupation of the day, when she could enjoy her morning coffee, and the scene outside her office window, without being involved with piles of paper work, visits for her Department here and there, her mind was making a clear of anything else gathering in it, which she was considering unimportant, and concentrated to what she thought it would be a good case, or an interesting one for her.

All day's work was not usually allowing that, voices from people on the telephone, colleagues and visitors in and out, letters, forms and demands, were forming but a long line of hundreds of other things she had to care about, no matter if sometimes she did not want to.

Like lots of other young women of her age, she thought little of having a future only with marriage and children, with a career sided in favour of them, with promotions harsh and scarce due to family obligations and ties.

A long time at work, the higher status that could be achieved, yes, very much yes to this, always in the picture, happy to follow and serve it.

Men were good fun, no doubt, but still enjoyable mostly entertainment for weekends, if not on duty.

As for children, Martha was sorting this out easily, and whenever a motherhood pang was surfacing, she could take her sister's children down to the west country to see the sea and play with them.

So, all matters arranged nicely and conveniently, time had only but one purpose, work and serving ambition. Martha had managed this efficiently.

Her background was poor. She was coming from a family with no income, other than next to basics for living, and no knowledge, other than some small for farming.

Her Suffolk village was pretty, but awfully boring, with next to nothing entertaining, and suffocating. Very young, her sharp mind indicated to her that these were no qualities for anyone who wanted to go ahead, and little Martha even on those long gone days, wanted but just that.

'The daffodils will be soon gone,' she thought, watching the exhausts of passing cars bathing them in pollution. 'The petunias might come up afterwards, and then what else?'

Tom, her assistant, got in and left a document on her desk. 'The 'Field Marshall' said that you should look at it carefully,' he told her, 'he says we should be more careful with foreign cases like this.' He left as he had come, closing very quietly the door behind him.

'That's it,' she advised herself, knowing that the end had come for any brain's rest and contemplation. She returned to her desk, placing the coffee mug on it, and picked up the letter.

She read it carefully, with only the occasional sips from her mug, then, she put it down and looked again at the letter. 'Asian art is high in demand,' told herself loudly, 'let's see it then.'

None of her family knew of art. The word had escaped their vocabulary, however Martha knew it, and she knew it well, as she liked and studied the subject, also it was the best vehicle to achieve her climbing of the ladder. Blood, theft, chasing criminals in cars, arrests, courtrooms, no, they were something for anyone else nearly in this Force, and for Martha the least she wanted to do.

Not a difficult person by nature, the element in which she was more comfortable was that of her steel character, which also cold and determined was serving perfectly the goals she had set for her. And those were no others than succeeding in a world, which was sophisticated and interesting.

She read again the letter with the strange symbols on top and marked with the capital letters in red ink, 'CONFIDENTIAL' and decided to deal with it with a rather quicker than usual way.

She left her desk and went to summon Tom.

'Do we know anything more about this?' She enquired.

'No, this is what 'Field Marshall' gave me earlier on, and he only said to be careful with it.'

'Why? Does he know anything more than what it is on it?'

'I have no clue, why don't you ask him?'

'I shall.'

She left him and walked down the corridor towards 'Field Marshall's office.

Superintendent Maximus Watfield was anything else but a 'Field Marshall', however this very short and thin man when he arrived at the Department, made with both his efficiency and knowledge, a huge impact on all of them. His system of demand, order, and work, twinned with his strange for an Englishman Roman name, provided him quickly with a nickname he also liked and enjoyed.

Martha could see but a small torso, nearly that of a child, on top of his desk, with a telephone in hand. She sat on the chair near him waiting patiently to finish his call.

'It's for the Chinese, isn't it?' He asked her as soon as he finished the telephone conversation and even before placing the receiver on its basis.

'Tom said that you wanted us to be more careful.'

'It's their government you see,' he smiled lightly, 'delicate case, they got themselves a little trapped.'

'Not very much I would say, it's not the first time that a crook steals items from a museum to sell.

'For some years though,' he cut her abruptly, 'they feel quiet embarrassed, and right now as the raising power that they are they do not certainly want to give any bad impression to westerners.'

'But it's a vast country, and from what it is here, this guy operated nearly everywhere.'

'Ah, a good policing system would have tracked down evidence sooner. It's sometime that this was going on, and it does seem that no one had any evidence.'

'Sir, it must have been really difficult, these were but small items only.'

'Important for their culture.'

'OK.' Martha had learned not to argue more with him. Sometimes it was easy to carry on with a case, however Maximus Watfield had a way to look at her and stop her in wishing to continue the argument. Martha though was not afraid of him, only counting on him for her own reasons.

'I think you have a quick case for the Magistrates, we need this warrant as soon as possible to go there and see what else he has.'

'There is a witness in this case, some Chinese cook, the

Embassy wants us to liaise with them before examining him, isn't that a little unusual, it should be independently?'

'That's all right, do it.'

'I 'll start then.'

'Good.'

'Field Marshall' had not much more time, Martha took the hint, the document, and left the room.

She returned to her desk, her cold coffee, whatever was now left in the mug, and the calls she had to start making. Then, she stopped and took her pen to write her official request to court.

The bulk of a fat body closed the opening left by the kitchen door.

Ching Lee continued to stir the pork on the wok, without turning around to look.

'What are you doing now?' Mickie's voice asked in its expected rude tone.

'You can see that, you don't need to ask me,' Ching lee replied, still not turning to look at him.

'What has happened?'

'About what?'

'Ah, don't be stupid, we had an agreement, where are the fans?'

'I have told you that I need some more time to find similar materials to those I need to repair. These are very old things, I work here nearly all day, I have but a small time to look in the shops for them.'

'You could have told me to buy you what you needed.'

Ching Lee turned now to look Mickie. He had a funny expression on his face with his lifted eyebrows, his eyes lit strangely, his lips half open, as they were all ready to explode into laughing, even before his mouth went into that.

'You wouldn't have a clue,' he said, finally with a big laugh.

'I would, if you had told me.'

'I couldn't, you have no idea of those things.'

'Mr Zhung wants them urgently, he keeps on asking about them.'

'Is his mother needing them again?'

'Don't play games with him. He told me to come and find you.'

'Why he wants them all of a suddenly so urgently? He said he wanted to repair these things to his mother's memory, what's wrong now?'

'I don't know,' Mickie scratched his head, truthful in ignoring Zhung's real intentions for the fans, or at least not being advised for the new deal.

Ching Lee returned to his cooking, retaining with some more effort now his outside coolness. He continued to stir the pork.

'Do you like some dumplings?' It was what he knew it could always work in destructing Mickie's attention.

'Ah,' said Mickie, joyful that after all this visit was not only following Zhung's instructions, but also his own wish too, which easily now had managed to see fulfilled.

Ching Lee opened the oven and took out a tray of freshly fried dumplings, he put few on a plate and left it on the table.

'Have these quickly before the boss comes here.'

'Ah,' said Mickie again, and approached the table with an animal's leap to catch its prey.

'Ching Lee turned lightly from the cooker to watch him.

'Does he not feed you well?' His voice joined the ironical tone in his face.

'Ah,' said Mickie, 'these are great, ah you do a good job,' either ignoring, or not catching the old man's comment.

'What shall I tell him?'

'What I told you.'

'It's sometime now that you have had them.'

'I have explained all about that already. If he likes he can have them back unfinished. It's up to him what he really wants me to do.'

'Ah, I will tell him that, but I gather you will see me again soon.'

'Do you like my dumplings that much?'

'Don't be funny, because he is not.'

'That's his affair.'

'I am off now.'

'Good bye.'

When Mickie had closed the restaurant's door behind him, Ching Lee switched off the cooker, transferred the wok to another hob and covered it, then he went to sit at the table searching his apron pocket for one of his rarely used cigarettes. His demons, all covered with his fears again, came back. He lit the cigarette, which luckily was there with another one, and some coins, and blew the smoke away. He could not hold on the fans a lot longer.

Quiet nervous about the whole affair, he got up again and went to open the door to the back yard. He stood there for few minutes, smoking his cigarettes, and looking vaguely at the raw of the already half full dustbins.

No, it would have not been easy to postpone for longer the delivery of the fans. Mickie was saying the truth, and he was sensing that not before long he had to face Zhung, and even the thought was making his stomach revolting.

He did not need a great imagination to understand that Zhung must have found some really good deal for them. His precious fans in the hands of someone, whoever, for pleasure, for fun, for money, for whatever, away from their glass cases, away from home, for good.

He stuck his eyes on the dustbins, which slowly started getting forms of elegant princesses, or beautiful courtesans, or some other lady of the aristocracy, perhaps even an empress, why not, that on a beautiful spring's day like this could take a stroll in a garden, where ponds were full with water lilies, butterflies would start flying away from the frost, the snow and the cold of the winter, as the earth and nature would start to revive again, when this unknown, imaginary beauty of her time, long now gone and forgotten, would hold one of his fans, moving it with grace in front of her face, as she was enjoying her stroll in the garden.

Suddenly she was lost again, and the big bulk of the grey and black metal bins, replaced her figure swiftly, and bitterly. And the fear came back to catch him.

What on earth was he doing? Did it really matter to him so much what it would happen to those items? It was not that great money that Zhung was giving him, nevertheless life had become because of that a little better, more comfortable than before. Why throwing all that away, what did he care for?

He could buy a toy or two for Abigail, some better stuff too to decorate her animals. She had been so happy with them now.

He smiled all too pleased to the thought of her smiling face, all those beads and threads, and new papers. How pleased she had been. How pleased he was he had made someone like Abigail smile.

He threw his half smoked cigarette recklessly to the yard, then it saw it landing at the side of a dustbin, and he went out to retrieve it and put it out properly.

'What a fool,' scorned himself for this attitude, and remembered Joy, making fun of him whenever he was seeing him smoking.

It was good that at last the boy and his mother had managed to return home. One or two cards were all he had received from him, telling him of the new job at the offices of a small company. 'Joy at an office,' he smiled.

Madame's Luo relatives had been quiet good to both of them supporting them a lot after Hu's death. Madame Luo had been very instrumental in stirring all this back home with her family. 'She was the good one,' Ching Lee thought of her, engaging his memory for a while to their lives.

He went back to the table, and retrieved his thermo flask, taking some sips from his tea there.

'It wouldn't have been bad to see them sometime again.' He did not host a great affection for Joy, whom he always thought as a hopeless case, always stupid and reckless, however they had always been the only people, his people really from those days back home.

The other Chinese here, some second generation already, some other small opportunists from Hong Kong, like Lao Ta, who had come here only for money.

He rested his eyes on the unpolished, hard wood of the table, whilst memories were flying all over him ahead of the next minute.

Hu and Madame Luo, knew of the real China, knew of its hard times, knew of its respect and agony. Nothing like that was with these others around now.

Ching Lee was seeing the Morton's on most Sundays, but this was only for Abigail's sake. Her smile, laugh, and happiness, when she had managed to make herself one more new paper toy, was the same pleasure and warmth in his heart, nearly as much as his fans had been. He had someone to care for, to love, to help forget any reality, and the reciprocal interest was leaving the taste of an unknown, or lost now in time, happiness.

He sighed, and putting his flask away, he got up to continue his cooking.

'How is it going with the Chinese case?' The"Field Marshall put his head from the door into Martha's office. Startled, she jumped up from her seat.

'We are nearly ready Sir. I think we will have the warrant from the Magistrates tomorrow, and we have advised the Embassy that we want to examine the cook.'

'Good, good, keep me posted.'

'Yes Sir.'

He closed the door again.

'You are wanted to the telephone,' Lao Ta announced to Ching Lee, looking at the same time at him suspiciously.

'Me?' He asked surprised from the cooker.

'Yeah, move now to get it, they will not wait for you forever.'

He switched off the cooker again, and wiped his hands.

His mind, connected still a little to Abigail's thought, suddenly panicked and rushed to the telephone in Lao Ta's office.

'I hope at least that the kid is OK.'

'Which kid?' Lao Ta asked, more suspicious than before.

'I am sorry I had to call you at the restaurant,' Wang's voice sounded clear and official from the other end, 'however I had to find you as soon as possible as Scotland Yard wants to ask you some questions. Don't worry about it at all, it's just routine, and we will go there together.'

'Me? Why me?' He asked, his fears now all around him for good.

'Well, you discovered the whole thing, didn't you? Anyway, it's for Thursday, the day after tomorrow,' Wang continued, 'can you be here at eight forty five? I thought to arrange the interview for earlier so you have time to go back to the restaurant afterwards. We should not raise suspicions, so please keep as quiet as you can about it. At least not now. You can make it can't you?'

Lao Ta had entered the room, and sat behind the table he was calling his desk.

'I suppose so,' said Ching Lee.

'Good, see you then.'

'Yes,' said Ching Lee, more as if he was replying for someone else than himself.

It was not that warm, not yet, despite all the spring's promises.

Martha looked at the short, old man, who was sitting nearly at the edge of his chair, looking mostly at the furniture and the carpet, than any of the persons in the room.

In her job she had come across hundreds of characters, which sprang from all levels causing her feelings and intentions, which were ranging from disgust to sheer admiration.

However, not this character. Her gut feeling for him was different, something like a very spontaneous kindness, which was covering his whole being, strangely reflecting back to those around, filling words, movements, everything.

His not very poor, but lost in time's oldness and hardy fashionable outfit, his quiet but extremely dignified manners, his slow but graceful movement, the low tone of his voice and general attitude, made even more difficult his classification in any of her known levels of human kind.

A small warmth sprang inside her and showed lightly on her small smile to him.

Tom, was looking indifferent, stupidly cold and professionally remote to the scene.

'Mr Ching Lee how long have you known Mr Zhung?' She asked him moving slightly her body towards him.

He raised quickly his eyes to look at her.

'The last few years he comes to the restaurant, we all know him, he is a very regular customer.'

'Does he come alone?'

'No, never alone.'

'Whom does he come with?'

'Various people, not the same each time.'

'Men or women?'

'Both.'

Anyone in particular that comes with more often?'

'His assistant,' he stopped for a while looking a little frightened as to provide her with more information. Never Mickie crossed his mind that he was anything other than a lazy, and stupid man, who was assisting Zhung for the reason that the job did not require any hard labour that he hated. However now he was asked about him, and he had to categorize Mickie as to the side he ought to stand for, a crook, or a man who just does a job to feed himself.

'Well?' Martha asked kindly, 'do you know the name of this man?'

'He is not an entirely innocent person you know,' Wang tried to help him with an annoyed smile, as he secretly found the whole story here as a waste of his time.

Martha looked at him a little angry. She had allowed him to be present because the old man wanted it, otherwise she was finding that any interventions from the Embassy's staff more irritating than helpful. She reassured himself that the 'Field Marshall's' decision to allow them to be involved, was not particularly helpful.

'Please Mr Wang.'

'I am very sorry,' Wang was quick to correct.

'Mickie,' said suddenly Ching Lee, who finally had decided about Mickie's placement to the bandits side.

'Mickie what?' Martha asked again.

'I don't know, that's all, Mickie, that's how we all know him.'

Martha went around her desk and sat in her chair. She took some notes in her note pad, and got up again soon.

'Does this Mickie comes often to the restaurant?'

'Before, he was coming with Mr Zhung, afterwards he started coming by himself too to bring me the items, or collecting those I had fixed.'

'Never to your house?'

No Ma'am, no one comes there, only to the restaurant.'

Martha went to the window and looked out at the square in the small distance.

More and more daffodils were dying day by day as springtime was progressing, giving their place to pansies and few hyacinths.

'In a while we will have summer,' she thought, 'how good, all this misery of cold ending at last.' She was looking forward to take her nephew and niece to the sea, swim, bath in the sun, do nothing for a while, or perhaps go with Tom to Thailand. Not exciting this, he was only serving as a part time boyfriend, when anything better was not coming along. However, he was not a bad companion for a trip abroad, better than her sister at least.

'Sometimes he comes irrelevant of Mr Zhung's items,' Ching Lee spoke all of a sudden, not knowing what of all information he had it should be given.

Martha turned from the window.

'To do what?' She asked.

'He likes my dumplings,' he told her timidly.

Martha looked amused.

'You must be cooking very well then.'

Wang smiled, 'He is responsible for increasing the weight of all of us,' he said.

'I wouldn't mind,' Ching Lee thought, 'if it was not for all those too frequent visits to the kitchen had not become but a habit.'

'I might turn up myself there,' Martha teased him.

'You would be welcomed Ma'am,' he told her.

Wang looked at his watch. It seemed to him that a more formal approach from the Arts Squad Inspector, might have finished earlier the interrogation.

He could hardly understand all these polite forms of

questioning, which to his opinion could hardly lead to their goal.

It was past eleven thirty when finally both men reached the door of Martha's office on their way out.

Ching Lee was speechless. He stood in front of the lift, hardly remembering, or fully understanding the reason as to why he had come to this place.

The men with uniforms around, the buzz of the offices and circulation of people, were giving him a terrorising feeling, as it was only now that his wishes for uncovering Zhung and saving his so precious items, were finally abandoning their place inside his brain or heart, and they were taking their shape into interrogating humans, forms, and endless questioning.

He was frightened, although regret for his actions were also mixing, sometimes unsuccessfully to some small, soothing thought that perhaps now his beautiful items might have a chance to find their correct place.

13

'Hello, hello, what are we having today?' Zhung had awaken cheerfully this morning.

He walked in his pyjamas to the kitchen clapping his hands with noise. He had managed to agree a good deal with an American collector last night for some items, and all it was left for today was to get Mickie to prepare them for delivery. It was a much better deal than he had hoped for.

'Your usual breakfast,' said Sue, emptying a fried egg and a couple of rashers of bacon from the frying pan she was holding to a plate on the table. 'I am stunned that you never have your own kind of food in the morning,' she told him.

'I love English fattening things,' he laughed and grabbed her bottom with joy that was watering his eyes.

'Mickie is around,' she warned him, not a bit disturbed.

'Who cares for that idiot,' Zhung's hand still stroking her buttocks, 'or you think that he doesn't know?'

'You think so?'

'I don't give a damn.'

He sat down and grasped his fork, sipping noisily tea from a cup in front of him.

The front door bell startled them both. They looked one another over the empty now frying pan.

'Mickie!' Mr Zhung shouted, 'look who is there on the damned door,' only to see few seconds later two policemen storming into the kitchen. Sue was still holding the frying pan.

'What, what is this?' He got up angrily from the table, 'what are you doing here?'

'We have instructions to search the house,' said Martha, 'Police Inspector Martha Nickolls, Arts Squad,' and she put her identification card under his nose, 'we have a warrant for this,' and she showed him a document.

Zhung's colour turned into a shade of tarnished copper. 'Why? What the hell is all this?'

'Possession of stolen items,' she advised him calmly, 'arts items from the museums of the People's Republic of China.'

'You must be mad.'

'I wouldn't be in a hurry to say anything if I was you Mr Zhung,' and she left the kitchen with two other policemen, making their way upstairs.

Sue was watching speechless, still not abandoning the frying pan.

One policeman stayed in the kitchen, 'you better sit down Sir,' he told him, 'you are not allowed to leave this room, not at least until the search is finished.

'Would like some coffee?' Sue offered, finding her voice in an effort to get out of this scene.

Zhung looked at her, full of anger and hatred.

'No, thank you,' replied the policeman, closing the kitchen door, and looking the space around for other exits.

Zhung sat upright in his chair, his narrow eyes darker than ever, fixed on the table and his food, which still remained intact in front of him.

Mickie was nowhere to be seen, at least this is what Sue and Zhung believed, stuck in the kitchen with the policeman.

However Mickie was already with the others, on the loft, where Martha had pushed him, ahead of her to open the door, which still and despite the efforts of another policeman, remained locked.

Mickie had no option. He had tried at first to say that only Mr Zhung had keys for this room, however Martha after the interrogation of Ching Lee, thought differently.

'If you co operate with the Police,' she had told him, 'it's

191

in your favour,' and Mickie believed her, and produced the keys. He would have done anything for not going back. He knew well that things back at home would have not been that easy for him either.

'Jesus Christ!' Martha and the two policemen stood aghast in the room at the loft, as soon as Mickie opened the door.

'Indeed,' said also one of the two policemen behind her, 'this is Aladin's cave, no doubt.'

Shelf upon shelf, floor to ceiling, and all around the room, were standing hundreds of items. Fans in boxes and without, mirrors, boxes, statuettes, scrolls, books, silk outfits, funeral vases, china, ivory animals, all in rows, each one wrapped in plastic.

'What else do you have here? In this house?' Martha addressed Mickie in anger.

'I don't know any more, I know nothing,' sweat was running down his cheeks like tears. 'I have told you everything I knew, Mr Zhung is in charge, he is the boss, I was just doing what he was asking me to do.'

'You were, didn't you?' She wanted so badly to kick his fat ass, his shivering oily face was causing her enough revulsion to do it gladly.

'Ah, 'repeated Mickie, 'I know nothing.'

'For the last time,' said Martha again, 'what else do you have in here?'

'Nothing, nothing, I already told you,' Mickie could not abandon the repetition he liked.

She noted to the other two policemen, who following her order rushed into the other rooms of the house to search and then, as their search produced nothing, after a meticulous turning upside down of all the furniture, cupboards, drawers, wardrobes, beds, everything, Martha noted to Tom standing behind her.

'Do you have a basement here?' Tom asked Mickie, 'or

you don't know about it either?'

Martha turned abruptly to look at him. At the moment and following his question, she considered him of equal wits as the assistant to Zhung.

'Why the hell am I with him?' She thought more desperate to her case, than what she had found here as she had not managed to get a better boyfriend, even for the few times that she wanted to play the role of the romantic woman.

Mickie did not reply.

'Of course they do,' she told Tom between her teeth, and showed him a small door in the hall, at the side of the staircase.

Tom, who had understood nothing, rushed to open it, but this door was locked too.

'I am certain you have that key too,' Martha said to Mickie, who right now would give the impression to an outsider that he was about to suffer an imminent stroke, as his face had a strange redness, and his expression was one of a totally confused and bewildered person.

He muttered something that no one could hear.

Tom pushed the door again. 'Your boss wouldn't like to have his doors broken, wouldn't he?'

He was about to explode crying as he was watching Tom to his third attempt.

'He is not good even for that,' the Arts Inspector thought for her boyfriend, 'he can't even brake a door. Steven!' She shouted to one of the other policemen.

The thick drops of sweat were coming down now Mickie's cheeks together with real tears. He felt lost. He knew that punishment from Zhung would have really been severe, but what could he do with all these policemen around? He had no hope.

Steve rushed down from one of the upstairs bedrooms.

Mickie as from a miracle took out of his pocket another

key, smaller this time and tied with a yellow ribbon.

'Well, let's see now,' Martha snatched it from his hands.

She opened the door and searched for a light switch inside. When she found it, she switched on the light, and second time around in one day, she stayed there in the middle of a room, amazed by what she had found.

The two windows inside were shut with dark blinds, whilst more and more shelves were displaying at the full length of the room items of extreme elegance and beauty.

In the twelve years she had been on the Force, she could have hardly remembered so many things in immaculate rows, the one next to the other, that were staying there, wrapped in cheap plastic, hidden from any light, waiting perhaps for an interested collector, or art dealer, even perhaps the occasional nouveau riche lady or gentleman, to be moved to a widow, a coffee table, or the occasional cupboard.

She could remember such exquisite things seen in museums, where with care and thought were waiting to be viewed by visitors, admired, discussed. However, never before she had a case, where such a number of so many beautiful things were waiting in the dark, like sheep for their turn of visiting the slaughterhouse.

The revulsion filled up her stomach.

She went up the few steps to the hall in a hurry, and stormed into the kitchen.

'I arrest you for possessions of stolen items,' she told to the man sitting at the table in front of his untouched breakfast. 'You have the right to remain silent,' Tom moved quickly to put him the handcuffs, 'anything you say it may be taken down and used as evidence.'

'The other two will follow us to the station,' she told Tom, 'get all these items out of here.'

Zhung, as if he suddenly was waking up from a slumber, jumped up from his chair.

'These things belong to my family,' he shouted, 'you have no right to touch them.'

'Let me see,' Martha put her finger in her mouth thoughtfully,' your father, or your mother, or perhaps your grandparents? Will you please inform me?'

'That's none of your damned business.'

'Really, isn't?'

She signed to get him out to the vans that were waiting outside the front door.

Zhung was moving his hands to get them out of the handcuffs, swearing all the time in Mandarin with anger, small amounts of saliva getting out from his mouth in thick drops, which decorated people, walls, and furniture around him.

'You have a musical language,' Tom spoke for the first time, wiping also his face.

At the hall Mickie had shrunk by the side of the staircase.

'You idiot,' Zhung shouted to him as soon as he set eyes to the his fat bulk, and the two policemen holding him, were pushing hard his still resisting body, outside. 'You always were an idiot, you had to betray me, didn't you?'

Mickie had shrunk even lower by the staircase, wishing more and more that he was dead than alive, his face like a trembling, big pumpkin, still sweating and crying.

'I will cut you into pieces, Zhung's eyes were two little, red lights.

'Ah, ah, it's the Police boss,' his voice sounded croaky and hardly getting out of his throat.

'Pleased you noticed it,' said Martha, and went around to take him too to the van.

Sue had not changed her position by the sink, her eyes moving only around, but her legs stuck all this time to the floor, as a doll fixed on a basis.

'You too Miss,' Tom approached her.

'Me? What have I done?' Suddenly she started getting in

touch with what was going on.

'We will soon find out,' and he took her by the arm.

More policemen came out from the second van with removal boxes and tapes.

One by one all the items from the basement and the loft, were carefully put into the boxes and transferred to the van, and when the van was filled to the top, a lorry arrived.

Ching Lee sat in front of the window in his small lounge, and watched the traffic outside.

Yesterday was a difficult day.

He had been thinking of it, again and again and again. During the time of his interrogation he was not frightened. Despite the fact that he had gone to Scotland Yard in panic, the woman there was kind to him, and after all, as Wang told him he was the good one who had uncovered the bad guy, and pay a good service to his country.

So they have said, nearly everyone there, but now though, away from the buzz and the people, the papers, the photographs, the questions, the story had started to unveil itself and taking different dimensions.

In some small, front gardens, among dustbins, weeds and some anaemic greenery, children were playing. The two men from across the road had stopped for a chat.

Spring was here now, it was for good and it seemed that it liked to stay for a while. The people had found other people, any small piece of earth they were possessing was planted with something, a smile.

The old demons had returned.

It had been OK so far. No fuss, no problems, no great moments, no distress, or joy, but only a flat, straight line of days, the one after the other.

He was scared of Zhung. He did not know how to fight these kind of people, he did not know how to fight anyone, only run, wasn't it after all what he was doing all these years, yet again, near now to the end, he was discovering that all those years inside the flat line, there was a voice hanging in the void of emptiness, his, he had not forgotten it.

The day yesterday was like those, all those years before, in his past, waiting in line at the Immigration Service. The Police, the immigration officers around, all those people of different colours, the endless queues, and the hours of waiting.

The same feelings, unknown, frightening, frustration and confusion, dressed up in words by those men and women full of questions. 'What have you come to do in this country? How long do you intend to stay? How much money you have? Where is this job you say you will work? What would it be your income?'

He didn't know how to face it then, he didn't know anything again now.

Bad people are bad people, you hurt them and they chase and flatten you, what more? Evil is evil and there is nothing you can do about it, nothing.

'Law? What law? Ah, the law of the other people, the good ones, yes the law, but this comes afterwards, it's always too late by then.'

He looked and looked outside the window before making the decision to get ready and go to work.

Wang had asked him yesterday, 'why don't you leave Lao Ta? I mean get a pension, you must have enough years for that.'

'Oh, yes Sir.'

'Then, have you given it some thought?'

'I didn't know I could do it, would that be enough to survive?'

Wang did not have a reply.

In his world of diplomatic allowances, no one knew how much an old cook can get, 'funny, how much really?'

'Do you reckon they can give me a pension here?'

'Where else?' Wang laughed, 'that's the only country you have been really working, isn't it?'

He didn't speak, but it was the truth, he really did not have the time to his own country to do that, how strange it sounded, all these years, here and only here, a country he still hardly knew that had been the only one he had some life.

'I think you should look into that. Lao Ta is not that generous, I would have thought.'

'No Sir.'

How good it would have been not to have to go there again, how happy to stay finally away from smells, pans, markets, dishes, Lao Ta above all.

He smiled again on the thought, as even and the illusion of such a new life with what he loved mostly to do, was already outside in the pavement.

Wang had promised though to look into that.

'He is a strange man,' Ching Lee thought, 'kind, considered, but full of ambition, not bad, people should have ambitions, he is young, he can afford it.'

Wang indeed had thought of him.

Inside his days twisting with information, building relationships with important people here for his country, and politics, there has been some space, small, but good space, for humans.

He knew that giving something creates something, and this span of feelings from satisfaction to compensation, materialistic as it might be, it stays inside and it's good.

The days of his father's struggles to do something, to leave to his children

with something better in life, had stayed inside him and had stained his future life with sentimentality. Pity was not exactly acceptable for Wang, perhaps goodness incorporated to a successful and ambitious business life, might have taken one further, who knows. And he didn't exactly know why, or cared about it, however at least he wanted to help Ching Lee, it didn't really matter for the rest.

The children in a while will empty the streets for their schools, the men and women will go, like him, to work, the house had started already to empty for the day. He had to get ready soon.

He went and opened a box, sitting inside a chest, his only chest in the house.

There, the one next to the other, the two fans, his precious, wonderful fans, were sitting, saved for good, perhaps forever.

He looked and looked at them. Like caressing a child's cheek before you will embark it for his or hers trip to that great school, somewhere far, which it will help it perhaps to be great, however it will take it away from you, he passed his fingers from their body, the wounds inflicted in it by time, or whatever else, now totally unseen, completely restored to their former beauty.

On the soft light of the morning, the figurines on the leaf, the ivory cleaned and shiny, the birds and butterflies coming alive out again, ready to move about in the room. He looked at them again, and again, and again. A long moment changed into minutes.

'I suppose I will have to take them to that Policewoman,' advised himself with sadness, 'perhaps now is the time. Will she look well after them? No more my beauties, I can do no more,' he said to them, and a tightness crabbed his chest, it would have not be the same if he could have taken them back to their museum in Nanking, his museum. 'You will never though be mine. For sometime, well, but you will go home, it will be good, back where you belong.'

He closed the box and placed it back into the chest, then

he took a card from the table with Martha's telephone number.

Abigail finished a small paper house she was making and showed it to her mother.

'Good, very good,' said Helen, lifting her head from the bowl that she was doing a mix for a cake, 'that's why I will let you have a big piece, you will like that, won't you?'

'You come to see it Mum?'

'I can do that from here sweetie, it's great.' She continued her job, deeply absorbed in her thoughts, pleased only that Abigail was doing better, however, things around had to be done, and as usually they had only her to do them. Besides, she had her other children to look after, it would not have been fair to deal with only one with not so much hope. Better, was only part of the story.

The ringing of the doorbell annoyed her even further, she left her bowl muttering and went to see who was calling. Now that the boys were in school and Berty at work, she would have liked to continue the day doing her job in peace, as this had been for long time a rarity, and whoever was there, could not have been that welcomed.

'I am sorry,' said Ching Lee, standing at the opening of the door timidly, 'I didn't mean to disturb you,' he looked at the flour on her blouse. 'May I show Abigail something? I think it will please her, and I saw that she has not left for school yet.'

'Hi there,' Helen offered a ready prepared smile, 'no, we kept her in today as she has some kind of cold, her nose is running and she has some temperature. But of course she will like to see you, she always does.'

'Thank you.'

She rushed to the kitchen and wheeled quickly her daughter to the sitting room, where Ching Lee was standing holding a box.

'Good morning,' he said to the girl.

'You will be fine here,' said to her daughter, 'you will excuse me though, I have work in the kitchen,' Helen was finally glad that Ching Lee will occupy Abigail for a while, leaving her in peace to do her job.

'What have you got in there?' The girl's eyes turned all too curious to the box he was holding.

'I wanted you to see some real fans,' he told her, when he was certain that Helen had returned to the kitchen.

'Yes,' Abigail said and her eyes became larger, sniffing at the same time.

He wheeled the chair to the table, and placed carefully the box in front of her.

'Do they look like mine?'

'Yes,' he said, 'but these are so beautiful. Perhaps you may make some like those one day, 'and he opened slowly the lid of the box. He removed the muslin that was covering them with care, he took them out, placed them on the table, and he stood there, more wrapped up with his feelings about them, than remembering for what he had brought them there for. He pushed the box away to give them more room, and smiled to them.

Abigail moved her eyes from the one to the other, and she stretched her hands to touch them. He saw her and shook himself as if he was waking up from a reverie.

'Careful, we have to be very careful with them.'

'Why can't I touch them?' She turned her eyes to him. 'Couldn't I touch them?'

'They are very old, very fragile. One day yours will be like those ones, if you will keep them for many years.'

'No, I won't,' she said vehemently, I want to touch them, to have them with me at my chair, they are mine, why can I not hold them?'

'Look,' he said, regretting a little already bringing the fans, 'the ladies who had them they were holding them of course and use them, but as the time goes the paper

201

becomes very sensitive, the silk also, all those things that are made from,' he stopped to see if she could understand.

Her brown eyes had stuck to his face, two small burning for learning coals, inquisitive and curious.

'That's why we put them in those places that we call museums.'

'Is it where mine will go?'

'Who knows, perhaps, if one day you will make funs as beautiful as these.'

'You did not look at my house, I will build houses, but I shall make fans too, I like them too, you will show me again won't you?'

'Yes,' he smiled, 'I will.'

'What happened to the ladies who had them?' She concentrated on the fans only now.

'They left.'

'Where to?'

'Oh, I don't know, another world I think.'

'Is there another world than this?'

'Perhaps.'

'Have you ever seen it?'

'No, but I will.'

'When?'

'Sometime, perhaps soon, who knows,' and he lost himself again between the girl's head and the fans on the table.

'Will you then come to tell me about it?'

'Of course,' he smiled, 'I will come to your dreams.'

'Do those ladies who had the fans come into yours?'

'Oh yes, they do, often.'

'Good,' Abigail clapped her hands, 'they have lots of people, look she said pointing to some figures, 'look on those ladies there on the bridge, you see? They have flowers around them, birds, 'she laughed, 'I have to make them too don't I?' She laughed again and sniffed more loudly.

'Abigail, careful don't do that, wipe your nose!' Helen's voice ended the scene.

'Yes, yes,' said Ching Lee, 'that will be good,' Abigail not knowing if he meant putting some ladies on a bridge in her fans, or wipe her nose.

'Do you like my house?'

He notice it for the first time, 'it's nice, sweet colours.'

'Ah, the flowers,' she returned back to the fans, 'what is this big flower here Mr Ching Lee?' She pointed to a flower decorating the guard stick in one of the fans, near the end of the leaf.'

'A lotus flower.'

'It's nice, yes? It's so nice.'

'Yes,' he agreed, 'I was certain then that you would like them.'

14

Ching Lee stood timidly in the middle of the big hall, wondering for few minutes where he had to go.

The appointment he had made on the telephone with Mr O' Connor was for nine thirty in the morning, and as usually for him he had arrived earlier.

Big and heavily built oak doors surrounded the hall. Their polished to perfection wood, as well as the fine plaster mouldings with wreaths of flowers that surrounded them, stunned him. He looked around in awe, some little agony still hanging inside him.

He was not used to do what he had come here to do. Life, in all it's ups and downs, small as they might have been, or sometime large as recently, had always the same blessing of the straight line. Suddenly, everything wanted to change. It was for his own good of course, no question about it, however it was new, and he was not young anymore to be excited and welcoming to anything. Age, which has fallen upon him, as it happens to most humans, has this suspicion for changes, any of them. The repetition of everyday occurancies, has had peace and reassurance, nothing wrong can happen then, and if it does, it's a rarity forming a shock, which you may incorporate in life, or not, but mostly it's quiet, and that's the most you can seek for these days.

Ching Lee continued to wander around, looking on things and people.

The Old Guildhall had very tall and impressive ceilings, the stucco mouldings on each of their corners following religiously the pattern on the panels of the doors with angels and wreaths.

It was an antique dealer he had come to meet.

Martha Nickolls, unusual for her usual behaviour, had

taken a special interest on him, she liked him. Was it for his honesty, or simplicity? She hardly bothered to find out, it might have been.

When everything was over with Zhung, and he was extradited with Mickie back to Beijing to stand trial, she had phoned him one day.

"Was he interested to repair some stuff for few known antique dealers she knew from her job?

He was frightened.

"Legally of course,' she had heard her voice laughing at the other end, as soon as she detected his fears.

'I could do with some extra money,' he had replied, 'winters are very cold and long here.'

'It's a deal then.' That's why he was here now.

He knew no one, and no one knew him. Ching Lee had never seen before all those beautiful things that were on display at all the stands. Some people were still setting more items around, in and out their booths, the fair had not yet started.

They had too many beautiful things here on display, everywhere, capable to take your breath away, he thought, furniture, pictures, glass, other ornaments. They too back home had lots of antiques, all he could remember, they had, he had not forgotten them. They were emperors stuff, some others from old aristocrats, which they thought that they should preserve them for posterity, 'museums, these were the places to put them so everyone can go to see them, here they are selling them,' Ching Lee thought that he did not like this very much. 'So many beautiful things, they can take your heart away.'

He looked vaguely for any fans finding nothing on display though. The Antique Fair was rather small, but exquisite. He walked a little more around, and then trying to kill more time he got out, to the big hall again.

He noticed people gathering there, obviously visiting the Guildhall for some other event, only few of them had some interest to peek through the open doors of the Antique Fair.

It was not only from old habit though that he had come here earlier today for his appointment, he was interested to watch people for a change.

All those years back at the 'Dragon's Head' he had little opportunity to do this. The people were only the customers, the staff, and then some neighbours back at home. Why not looking at all these people now, those new faces, expressions, gestures, attitudes, manners? It was fascinating. Time was not a problem anymore.

It was good to watch people, to study them. Their faces and bodies carry stories around, betray lives. He was not considering it as an intrusion, you care for them, what more they can tell you other than words. Of course they do keep things tightly locked in their hearts, or brains, that was entirely their affair, but how a glance, a gesture, a breath can give away, that is fascinating to observe.

It was awkward at the beginning to have time for anything. He really did not know what to do with it.

Wang had helped him to get a pension, more, he rather took action to organise it to detail, strange, but also that military guy at the Embassy, colonel Zhao assisted him.

Of course Wang had been the great beneficiary of the story, with an excellent promotion on the pipe line for the Ministry of Foreign Affairs as spokesman on foreign policy, or Head of some Department, for the young boy of Mr Luo things have not gone badly at all.

Even Berty had told him that it was a good idea. 'Why on earth to let this man take more of your life mate? Don't you thing it's time to do something for yourself?' And he had done it.

But time? What one is doing with it?

He had become even more meticulous with his fans. He stored them more carefully, and wrote notes for their provenance and materials. He bought a notebook and he started writing about repairs and restoration of fans. Then, every Sunday it was Abigail, whose dexterity and skill on crafting toys on paper had made her feel so much better everyday. Helen had found already some small shops around buying them, Abigail had been so happy when a radio station had come around when they found out from her school about this special talent of the girl.

Doctors and teachers were satisfied, and poor Berty smiled now ever so often watching her struggling with the colourful papers all around her.

Abigail was a fast learner, and Ching Lee had deeply rooted inside him now this special feeling for her. Was she the grand daughter he would have never had? Who knows, sometimes bonds in life are stronger with strangers than with those with blood connection.

Now and then he was thinking about all those things. Time has blessings too, you remember yourself, talk to him, consider feelings and ideas, it was not all a waste.

Then it was the money. His pension was not anything great, but neither salary from Lao Ta had ever been, perhaps now he was even slightly better off.

The women that were gathered in the hall, made an impression on him. The strange scarves that had around their necks, the funny jewels, which on occasions were huge metal disks, or beads, the potato sacks shapes and sizes of their weird handbags, which were sometimes decorated with animals, flowers, or symbols, their strange, haughty faces, with an air of pretentiousness, which was making them to look so empty and cold, as a glass bowl.

He never enjoyed much watching women. As species right now were leaving him uninterested, he only was watching the humans, no more.

The pang for a woman's company, her touch or feel, had been drawn through thousands of days and nights all that long time ago inside him. It had stopped with the betrothal to Pang-Mei.

Times around, when he had first come here and he was seeing the face of a pretty woman, he was in a hurry not to be seen that he was looking, his eyes quick to disappear on the pavement, on the road, or the floor of the tube carriage. Later, at night when their memory was coming back to him, he could enjoy their faces alone for few minutes, no more, after that sleep was always coming to rescue him.

What had he retained from him as a man? Not a lot. Now, for all those forty years nearly, he had only been a human being, no more, no less.

Sexuality had been but an instrument of the body, you may suppress it, or if you are strong to ignore its functions. He always believed that, there had been times that advice to himself was easier given than done, and for those cases there was Hu always not so far to assist with the occasional lady at the massage parlours in the back streets of Soho.

But now, all these women around seemed so strange, as even and the lot of them was demonstrating something, which did not exist, or ever existed.

Their little laughs like small cries of birds, sounded neurotic, short, cut off of any feeling of joy or other, which might have provoked it.

'Silly,' if there is something about them he told himself, looking also at his watch to see if the time for his appointment was approaching, 'that's what they look like and behave, silly.'

Satisfied that he had completed his curiosity on them, he returned to the room where the Antique Fair was taking place to find the man that Martha had suggested to meet. Mr O'Connor was a middle age, short and fat man with a spiky moustache and beard. His clever blue eyes seized Ching Lee quickly and thoroughly, but as soon as the examination was over, he smiled broadly to him and shook his hand warmly. Ching Lee found his attitude genuine.

'Inspector Nickolls,' started Ching Lee timidly.

'Yes, yes,' O'Connor quickly interrupted, 'thank you very much for coming here, you see I should have come to see you, but with this Fair here, I am tied up, and I only have an assistant at the shop.'

'No, no,' Ching Lee moved his hand in joy of saving himself from the prospect of having a visitor at the flat, 'no, it was an interesting pleasure for me to come here, I can see new things I did not have the time to see before, a good destruction you see.'

'Ah OK then, please sit down,' and he showed him an elegant chair at the back of the stand, whilst he sat to the twin one opposite.

Ching Lee watched him in horror expecting the beautiful item to collapse under the bulk of his body.

O'Connor read smiling his thought, 'they are strong things these you know, they had good craftsmen then to make good furniture.'

'Yes Sir, indeed, it was the same too in our part of the world.'

'Oh I am sure, I have seen pieces of your furniture that amazed me from their fantastic making, all those years ago, it's great.

Now, let's see what you can do for us,' he watched his watch too and the doors, aiming to finish any agreement, or discussion with the old man before the public started to come in. 'I have few fans I would like you to repair and of course value them for me, you reckon are of any interest for you? I also found some textiles, and a dagger, I want to have them perhaps, say taken care of, is that OK by you?'

'Of course, of course Sir.'

'Look, I believed you would have liked to see those items, but unfortunately I don't have them here, they are at our storage, so I will get my assistant to bring them over to you in one of those evenings, if it's possible, we can do it after we close the shop.'

'Oh no, no Sir,' Ching Lee's panic return on the prospect of having visitors in the flat, 'I can go and see them myself at your storage, perhaps collect them even, from your assistant. You know there isn't much to do outside these days and I don't like staying indoors all day, so I like to grasp any opportunity,' he smiled humbly on that, 'to give my old bones a walk.'

'Are you sure? We are in Mayfair, is that all right for you?'

'It will be no problem, I know my way around London you know, being here around forty years.'

'That long,' Mark O'Connor contemplated for few minutes, 'you must have come here then during those years of the mad youngsters destroying everything around.'

Ching Lee paused in silence, never he liked questions of the kind, now though he realised that being out there and working with other people in this country questions of the kind could have come perhaps more often, and they were unavoidable.

O'Connor was regretting his intrusion.

'I am sorry,' he said, 'none of my business.'

'Yes,' replied Ching Lee, 'that was the time indeed, my family was perished, all of them, I had nowhere else to go, I came here from Hong Kong.'

'I am really sorry for that.'

'It's OK, but I am sure that the Inspector must have told you about me.'

O'Connor showed to be a little embarrassed, 'yes' he agreed. 'Well look now,' he hurried to continue from before, 'it's a deal then, how about Friday, say six o'clock in the afternoon, so John would have finished with any clients, and he can discuss things with you.'

'It's fine Sir, I will be there at six, please give me only the address.'

O'Connor got up and fetched quickly a card from a box. Ching Lee took it and got up to leave him. The problem of how to price them was going around his mind, still though he was indecisive to ask, trade had nothing to do with him, the only relationship with all those stories of repairs in his life had, was none other that fans were items he adored. However, and for a second time O'Connor read his mind.

His sharp eyes had already searched the old man with whatever he wanted to know, and they had provided his mind with information he liked. He was a decent creature, timid and honest, and from what Martha had told him, a rare repairer of fans. He very much had liked this, perhaps more than his other attributed qualities. You could not have looked any further. In his profession really talented craftsmen to repair such exquisite old items, were few and scarce. It had been an excellent idea after all to retain such a good relationship with Inspector Nickolls. She could also come up with information of the kind, or other things of interest to him, and he could always supply her with bits and pieces of intelligence she wanted.

'Look,' he said again to the old man, 'you don't have to worry about a price on the repairs.'

'I am never unreasonable,' said Ching Lee, 'besides I have to see everything and estimate the amount of work I have to, plus materials. These are not easily found anymore.

'It's OK. We will sort out whatever you might ask, don't worry on this.'

Ching Lee had a feeling that he had started to like the man. His over bursting personality, had an air of goodness, or better a lack of shrewdness, which he always disliked.

O'Connor offered him his hand, which was taken and shaken with a mutual feeling of partnership.

'Good luck with the Fair,' Ching Lee told him outside the booth.

'We need that, business you see it's not flourishing so much these days as it used to be. We lost the Americans you see, and their dollar gets weaker and weaker. Gone you see are the old days, scary things nearly all of them do not like so much these days to come back to Europe, few only dare to do it.'

Ching Lee amused himself silently about how many times O'Connor was using the verb 'to see,' but he kept it inside.

A bunch of women in the hall outside peeped from the open, entirely open now big doors, to have a look at the Fair.

Ching Lee turned timidly to O'Connor again, 'may I ask you, if you know of course, what are all those women waiting outside? I am sorry for the question, however I thought that were looking a little odd, pardon again my curiosity, it might be I think my absence for years from the outside world.

Mark O'Connor burst into a heartily laugh, which bounced his jaws making the spiky hair in his beard to protrude even worse.

'Sophisticated cows my friend,' he continued laughing, 'it's a literary event you see over there, and they think perhaps that some of them are lost literary figures of the country just because they wrote some verses back at school.'

His laugh died out slowly, but he was still looking quiet amused sharing with the other the oddness on which they had both agreed about them.

'God help their husbands, if they have any that is, which I doubt, to have them recite Wordsworth in bed, 'his laugh started again, but in a lower tone now, he was concerned slightly that he had gone a little far with this old stranger.

'Thank you,' said Ching Lee, it has been a pleasure meeting you.'

'The same here.'

He strolled a little more around admiring some of the exhibits, and then left the Guildhall. There have been no women outside anymore.

He walked for a while the streets around, carefully navigating himself not to lose the tube station he had used, and he thought that day by day the old world he was now slowly exploring, it had started to have a better face.

Despite the fact that it was September, the weather was still warm, and very pleasant. Some kind of sweetness was in the air, where nothing was too warm, or too cold, but just so perfect for everyone's taste. As even and the weather had finally reached this extraordinary balance among all humans and their desires, something which could have been otherwise so impossible, that now with this harmony had nearly reached the miracle.

The kids, new school uniforms on, were lingering around returning from their lessons, playing, laughing, devouring their fast food from the badly smelling oil paper bags, or just hanging on pavements with their friends, enjoying every bit of the day before returning home.

It had not rained since August, and everyone was trying, whilst it lasted, to profit from it.

Abigail had a red hat on which a rather large daisy was decorating its front.

She had made it especially for her hat, and even Helen did not have the heart to tell her that it was too large for it. She was sitting quietly in her chair, at a sunny spot, turning the pages of book with photographs in her lap.

Helen, next to her, was stretched on a deck chair, eyes closed, almost grateful for once for being able to be away for a while from her worries, problems, and everyday tasks.

Regent's Park had been busy with people like them, who wanted to push back even the memory of an autumn and winter already coming to their threshold.

Ching Lee returned from the mobile canteen holding lemonade, an ice cream, and a tea for him.

It had been his idea to Berty that Abigail needed to get out more from the rather dark misery of their flat, and enjoy some more light, sunshine, and perhaps the idea of a garden around her. Berty had agreed, always quick to recognise any matter that could have been beneficiary for his daughter, even if he had not thought of it, however being at work all day, he could not help.

Helen had rejected primarily the idea, moaning as usually that all the hard work was left for her, and what about the boys. Right now though, bathing in the sunshine, and thinking that it had been Ching Lee manoeuvring Abigail's chair around, paying for the taxi, and fetching the drinks, the idea seemed not a bad one at all.

The book on Abigail's lap it was one about China, and full of photos. Pagodas, gardens, palaces, rivers and gorges, gods and warriors, ladies and fans, fans, and again fans to see in all their beauty, and exquisite artistry, was fascinating her.

One more present from her old friend, it had been both stimulating and educating her with the history on photos of a land, that she would never have any chance of visiting, and yet again a country that she already knew from his stories and loved so well.

Ching Lee gave Helen her lemonade, Abigail her ice cream, and sat himself on the grass to drink his tea.

'You are now shorter than me,' Abigail laughed at him, and he smiled back at her comment, all her good hearted little jokes melting in his chest, where before in that great passage of time, no any other human being had a place.

'Say thank you Abigail,' Helen's voice always could find a way to intervene.

'Thank you,' said the child, returning to her book, her smile lost.

'I thank you,' Ching Lee smiled broadly to her, 'for coming with me to the park, and keep me company, otherwise I would have been totally alone, and even the birds, and the squirrels would have been sad to see me sitting here by myself, and they would talk the one to the other. So, you see how grateful I am to you?'

Abigail's smile returned more broadly than before, she had completely understood that the bond between them it had been still there, it would have always been there, and the old man would always know and understand her. Her small age, and disability had been no impediment in seeing the truth around her. Her antennas all the time were out there to receive even the smallest amount of love, understanding, and compassion. Her little brain perhaps had grown enough through sadness and isolation, to see that she had been and will continue to be a burden to her family. With the exception of Berty and Elliot, and their small breaks of joy that were giving by dealing with her and her problem, Helen and Thomas did just what a duty requires, no more no less.

She was still too young to understand how adults feel, if she was not, perhaps she could have seen Helen's pain every time she was watching out a girl jumping and playing in her daughter's age, and as for Thomas, boys are boys, some care some not, all is not the same. Ching Lee though was something totally different. His tired, skinny and full of veins old hands had taught her joy, providing colour, usefulness, dedication, purpose, happiness.

As happiness has some times this very difficult perception by humans, they all wait for the big things to come, touch them, and hold on to them forever, and during this so many little moments of it come and go undetected, unrecognisable, unappreciated, lost, just because they are nothing other than small things of stupid nothings, which come and leave without any fuss.

'Who is this lady here Mr Ching Lee?' Abigail put her finger on the photo of a stiff, older woman covered in jewels, with few ladies around her, all wearing big earrings, and having in front of her feet four Pekinese dogs.

Ching Lee stretched his head from the ground to look at the photograph in the book.

'Ah, that was out last Empress, the Dowager, we used to call her 'The She Dragon.'

'Was she a real dragon?' Abigail opened her eyes more widely.

He laughed, 'in a way she was a great dragon, but not like those with wings and big, wild eyes that you see in the books, but with her brain, her will.'

'She was not good then, was she?'

'I agree with you, she was not that good, but China you see it's a vast country, in those days you had to be very powerful to govern.'

'And did she govern?'

'Yes, for a very long time. Have I ever told you her story?' Abigail moved negatively her head.

'Well then,' he said and putting himself in a more comfortable position in the grass, had a sip from his tea and started.

Helen thought that this was a good time as any to have a nap.

15

And the autumn appeared one day, quietly and without any fuss. Suddenly the blue of the sky turned white by all that gathering of clouds, which at first showed peacefully travelling the sky, before they turned into grey, and black, and the first rain in really two months, started to wet pavements and roads.

Fewer and fewer were the people out in the evenings, whilst nestling back home after work, became the normal again.

Gone were the groups of people gathering in the afternoons out in the pub for a drink, to enjoy the last sunshine, for as long that was lasting, gone and the children in the pavements and roads, gone the mothers with the push chairs in the parks, the young girls screaming, half drunk at night, and the willingness of all humans to get out and do more promptly their everyday tasks for whatever purpose those were.

The local news on the television had shown Abigail wearing a new silk, green dress, with a small butterfly sewn near the neck, as she was cheerfully talking to the presenter of the programme about the paper animals and other toys she was making, and her paper fans, which 'Mr Ching Lee' as she said, had taught her to make too.

Helen told the old man, that the producers would have liked to include an interview with him as well, but he had declined politely.

'It's Abigail's day,' he told Helen, 'why deprive her of that joy, after all I am too old for that sort of thing.'

Helen had made no comment, and finally here she was, her little daughter alone on the television, a little star, 'I think that Mr Ching Lee has told me, that what I am doing is called origami, or something like that.'

Berty's face was lit up with joy as he was watching her behind the cameras, and Helen had also a dim smile hanging over, as finally she had something little to be proud of her daughter.

Thomas and Elliott were pushing elbows at the sofa, watching the television, whilst Ching Lee, who was left at the Morton's house unwillingly to supervise the boys, sat quietly at his chair.

Only Elliott said rather without a lot of thought at the end of the news, 'it's good for her.'

'Yes,' had agreed the old man, and then the boys quickly switched the television to a programme about football heroes.

It was a small break from the rain for few minutes now, but no one knew how soon it would have been before it would start again.

The café was a small one, but well positioned on top of the canal at Maida Vale road. There was no one there but him, and a young couple at a corner, hardly noticing anything else other than themselves, their coffees left to be cold for sometime now on the table.

When he had come earlier on this morning to find shelter from the bucketing rain outside, he was pleased to find out that the café was nearly empty on this Sunday. He had been walking for more than two hours, rarely pushed by any weather to avoid this habit, but suddenly the sky had turned the slow, continuous rain that it had before, to a storm.

It was him and the vast city, and it had been so for all those thirty nearly years, and this strange bond of indifference in both, to unite them.

There will never be any love between them, he thought about it so many times, he did not belong here, and the city did not know him.

Yet again he knew nothing else but its roads, the

pavements he had been walking on, and he continued to do so, the pale and scarce sunshine in the winter days, the rare, soaring with damp, heat in the summers, the promising mornings of the spring, and the endless rain, at nearly all times.

And he had nothing else but this city to nourish, feed and keep him. The humans, no matter how friendly and good they have been, they had only but themselves.

Humans are lonely creatures, they are born alone, they die alone. He knew that, he had been sensing it deep into his bones, even from those days of his youth in Nanking. He had not stayed behind to help anyone, or die with them, each one of them had faced the end on its own, the father by the mob of youngsters, the mother and the girls as the flames were surrounding them. Everyone alone.

A little barge ignoring the bad weather and rain, went down the canal, a man at the stern with a dark cloak and hat, steering it steadily.

'Would you like some cake?' The voice of the café owner startled him from his thoughts.

'Or a croissant perhaps? They are very fresh, the guy who supplies the hotels nearby, drops some for me too.' Ching Lee looked at him making an effort to understand what he was asking.

He had not eaten since last night, and despite his austere food habits, his stomach was giving him pangs now, which before the man asked him for food, he intended to ignore.

'Perhaps the later,' said timidly, still finding difficult to order alone anything.

'A croissant then,' said the man and grasped a big one from a glass container and put it swiftly to plate with a small jar of jam and butter, before bringing it to Ching Lee's table.

He had chosen the one at the middle of the window, facing the canal from where he could watch any passing barges and the houses around. When the food landed to his table, he watched it carefully, a complete western treat for one's morning. He shrug his shoulders not knowing what to think about it, however he cut a piece from the croissant, and opened the small jar.

Carefully, and with neat movements he took a piece of the soft jam and spread it evenly on the croissant.

He was amused with himself as a child who manages first time to eat alone. The battery taste of the croissant accompanied by the sweetness of the strawberry jam went down pleasantly.

'I might buy some of these to have at home,' he thought, 'perhaps Abigail likes them too, they will be good to have them before school,' he continued to amuse himself with this discovered taste, the café owner watching him with idle curiosity.

'I was right, wasn't I?'

He agreed with a movement of his head, not wishing to indulge the other into some carefree conversation, just because there were no other customers around.

Besides, he wanted to linger over this new thing that it was for him to have a westerner's breakfast and liking it. All these years working at the 'Dragon's Head' he had remained religiously Chinese, not only in habits, but food too.

May be it was for all those Chinese people at the restaurant. He stopped eating and rested his eyes at the dark waters of the canal.

'I start coming out,' he thought,' as a tortoise out of his shell when he is not afraid of any danger any more. All those years for a place to live and some food, only that,' and something as a hard knot stood on his throat. 'All those years, lost, gone, not knowing anything.'

'Awful weather,' said the owner undeterred.

'Yes,' he agreed again in a low voice.

'Any more tea?'

'No thank you, I have already enough.'

'It will go on like this all day.'

'We should not complain, we had good weather longer than in other years,' said Ching Lee, and put one more piece from the croissant into his mouth, determined now that the necessary exchange of weather news had finished, to close the conversation. In support of this, he turned completely his head towards the canal, pretending he was watching carefully the barge, which now he could hardly see through the mist.

He watched instead few people coming out of the church on the left, closing their umbrellas, 'good, the rain it's obviously finished, at least for a while,' he thought, and rushed to swallow quickly the remaining of the croissant and the jam, drink his tea, and get out. After all he had only come to get some shelter from the downpour, and did not want to disturb his Sunday morning walking ritual, which for years now could not have given up for anyone, or anything.

He took the bill to the counter and paid.

'Are you from around here?' The owner asked again on the hope that he might catch a regular.

'I live in Camden,' said Ching Lee.

'Ah,' said only the other, already disappointed in losing on the prospect.

'Good bye,' said Ching Lee.

'Cheers,' replied the café owner, wiping the area around the sink at the back of the counter with a sponge.

The couple at the corner continued fondling the one the other, noticing no one and nothing around.

'They will stick here with only one bloody coffee,' the café owner looked at them in despair, carrying on with his job, and with little swearing between his lips for the rainy weather.

Ching Lee decided to walk across the canal, towards the bridge at the end. He liked the area, the pavements lined with plane trees, the stucco houses.

At the other side the members of the catholic congregation, were leaving the church, few walking towards various directions, but most of them going to collect their cars.

'No one walks these days,' Ching Lee shook his head watching them. The damp was penetrating him, and he tightened his raincoat around his body. He had bought a new one.

O'Connor had given him several repairs to do, but his fans were western ones, mostly made in France, few in Germany and in this country, the last two centuries.

Ladies in crinolines, men in wigs, little dogs, bridges, some flowers. Ivory guard sticks, or mother of pearl, that kind of thing.

'Not great, not bad,' he had thought, when he studied in Canton they were told that it was there that they started producing them in greater numbers for export, 'they copied us afterwards in the West, and still cannot make them as we had done, just imitations, without the touch of time and the good materials used on them, they would not impress.'

There had been though two of good craftsmanship, despite being European, which he admired. He had put himself down to work on them, he used to work now in all the weeks days, when he had something to repair, again rising early in the morning, as nothing should be changed from his old routine.

Things must not change, everything was well when only the line of days remains totally undisturbed. Changes are for the youth, but now it was better this way.

O'Connor was happy with him. Ching Lee's first impression of the man had been correct. He was an honest man, always with good humour, paying well without any grumbling. He had also introduced him to some more of his colleagues, so work was more than frequent, and he was very pleased with that.

Nothing great of course, but more comfortable days that he had to see since he left China, and time. That great luxury of time, and be a boss to himself only.

He had managed to change a little the darkness of his flat, Berty introduced him to a colleague of his, that used to be a decorator before he moved into removals, and he had freshen up the rooms with new paint, which have not been touched in years. He had chosen nice, soft colours, and one could say that they were looking a bit pretty now. Price, his landlord, had been happy about it, as he was always interested in collecting rather than spending money in the flats.

He had even hung new curtains, Helen had found the fabric locally, and sewn them for him. 'She was very kind 'he thought. 'She is a strange woman, always polite to me, a nice mother for the boys, and yet again, so many times, Abigail seems like a burden to her. Should mothers always be proud of their children? Why not just be happy that they have them? Strange, strange woman.'

The flat had been now a working place that he liked to be in. As soon as he finished with the restaurant, and started getting some more money from O'Connor and the other antique dealers, he had thought to move out, however he knew the people there, and whilst the house had started gradually to run down, mainly due to Price greediness, its current tenants were not too bad. Then, they were the Mortons of course and Abigail.

'We might move together if things get better, 'Berty had told him one day when the matter was discussed. He had smiled, 'I am not going to be a burden to anyone,' he had said.

'Eh, mate, you are like family to us, we owe you a lot, Abigail's life changed completely, she is a normal kid now, I mean apart from her disability. Honestly, you have been great, like a grandfather to her, a real one, since our fathers Helen's and mine, died long time ago. I don't know how you managed to get out all these things from the kid and changed it.

'No,' he said, 'you owe me nothing, I did nothing for Abigail, she had it at all times inside her, it was simply waiting to find a voice, I only helped her to find it.'

'Nonsense, nonsense, you are too modest mate.'

Berty disagreed giving him a hug, and Ching Lee immediately had forgotten any thoughts of moving.

Wang had suggested that perhaps he should have liked now, that things were in order, to go back, visit China for a while, see Nanking, which he would not recognise as it changed into such a beautiful city.

'It always had been,' he replied, 'cities do not change, we do it for them.

He had refuge to do it, even when Wang promised that the Embassy could pay for the ticket there.

'Seeing whom? What, what is there for me now in China? Everything is gone, and gone forever.'

Wang insisted in offering help to investigate few things about his family, or perhaps any relatives that had survived, didn't he have there anyone that he wanted to see?'

He had thought of Pang-Mei, but she would be old now like him, married surely if she was alive, with children. Was she alive? What might have happened to her and her wealthy family?

He had looked lost in Wang's desk for some minutes. How many times at night he was awake thinking of her, of all of them. But what would have been the purpose of going back now, for what purpose he should have known about the exact way they were all perished, those who did, or survive those who managed it. No, he would never go back, he was too old for more sorrow, besides he would know no one, and no one would know him.

'I think that you have been too much anglicised now,' Wang had laughed, seeing that there was nothing more he could do.

'I will never be,' he replied him, 'I am only an old Chinese that has left home. You have no idea what I have been carrying all these years, nothing, you don't have a clue who really I am, and what I have here,' and touched his chest.

And the way he had said it was nothing more that such a painful and simple reality, that Wang stopped laughing and never suggested it again.

'Besides,' he had thought, 'I do have someone here, someone I care for and she cares for me,' but he never told Wang.

Walking now by the canal, he smiled on the thought of the girl as she had seen in the new green, silk dress he had bought for her to appear on television, or the huge hug she had given him, when she Berty and Helen returned her home from the TV station.

It had been a strange bond the one he had with this country, or better this city. It was like a feeling of pending between worlds, vacillating as a pendulum, however it was now like things were concluding somewhere, and the sad and uncertain feeling of belonging in neither of these two worlds, had suddenly changed, landed somewhere, found some ground to rest.

Was then this his city after all? It would have been so difficult to answer.

He had reached the bridge and saw to his right the Warwick Avenue tube station. Perhaps he should have returned, have a bit of rest and prepare his Sunday lunch, then he would see Abigail in the afternoon, they were doing some history together now. No complains, it would be a full day again, it was not bad and lonely anymore.

Sometimes he was going back to Chinatown to do his shopping now on Chinese ingredients for his meals, and seeing Ami then, get from her few news for the people he knew, but he never went back to see anyone at the 'Dragon's Head.'

With Joy and madame Luo now back in China, little he cared for the others. They had always been an indifferent lot at its best, no it was better to close that door. However, the long time at the place was not helpful in getting easily accustomed to the idea that life was there no more, old habits die slowly but not giving their place to others as they go.

Bits and pieces of the sky started to show as few clouds started to withdraw.

He decided that he did not want to go home as yet, he crossed the bridge, and directed himself towards the other side, where the canal was forming some kind of harbour with more barges mooring there.

He had little to care about anything anymore, after all no one was waiting anywhere for him, no one except Abigail. He smiled to that, and felt content at her thought, a granddaughter, a little friend to care for and take care back for him.

She had even noticed his new raincoat the other day. 'Good,' she had told him, 'it's nice, I like it,' and he had blushed like a schoolmate of hers.

He was filled with her thought, then it was Berty, who insisted to get him out one Friday evening and take him to the pub with him, and O'Connor, who invited him to join his family at one weekend at their country house at the Cotswolds. 'It's beautiful there, you will like the English countryside, very green,' he had told him. He had never seen it, other for few old journeys at the past, working out of London for a while.

Some of the barges had pots with geraniums, lots of them, all over their decks. It was a pretty thing to see, even now in grey days like this.

The long line of stucco and brick houses, whose red colour had come to enhance the white and green around, the black iron railings separating the properties from the pavements and the road, the big windows allowing the light, whichever left, to penetrate the rooms.

It had come very slowly, very calmly.

He was sitting at a low fence watching the moored barges swaying in the light wind, when he felt it.

It was a quiet, long, filling him all over, feeling.

This after all was his city now.

He had but this city, and every street, every corner and pavement belonged to him, he had a right to call his together with all those other millions of people, who breathed and lived here. Things have changed, had changed a lot since he knew them, but neither Abigail, nor Zhung, or Wang and O'Connor, had managed to achieve in making it to look different for him.

It was nothing else, and no one else to contribute to this, none other but this vast, not pretty anymore, inhuman, and still so much loved, faceless city.

He belonged here now.

The damp had reached his bones, and he tightened even more the raincoat around his body for warmth.

Nanking had fled away, with its houses, lake, river, museums, mausoleums, temples, markets, people. It fled away with pain, with blood, with death and flames. Nanking was no more.

He got up slowly and walked to the edge of the pavement watching the black waters of the canal, his eyes fixed on them.

It was as even Nanking had been just drawn there forever, a city under the water and nothing more.

'I have to return,' advised himself, and turned back moving slowly towards the Warwick Avenue tube station.